James Matthews left school at 13, knowing that he wanted to be a writer. A teacher once gave him 101 out of 100 for an essay and pinned it to the classroom wall.

He has been involved in most phases of black writing in South Africa since its first flowering in the 1950s, and is currently active in the Congress of South African Writers. His own writing has an authority drawn from being black in present-day South Africa, and has led to his being detained without trial.

THE
PARK

and other stories

James Matthews

Longman

Longman Group UK Limited
Longman House,
Burnt Mill,
Harlow, Essex
CM20 2JE, England
and Associated Companies throughout the world

First published by Blac Publishing House, 1974

Second edition Ravan Press (Pty) Ltd 1983
This edition published by Longman Group UK Ltd 1989

ISBN 0 582 04080 9

Produced by Longman Group (Far East) Ltd
Printed in Hong Kong

*This one is for Jimi, Quinton, Terry, Jason,
and not forgetting Ché*

Contents

The Portable Radio   *1*

Incident   *11*

The Man Who Was Too Small   *16*

Whites Only   *25*

Mistaken Identity   *34*

Baby, That's the Way It Is   *41*

The Homecoming of Mr Brown   *51*

Tribute to a Humble Man   *65*

Colour Blind   *72*

Bitter-sweet Memories   *81*

Crucifixion   *91*

The Awakening   *105*

Three-way Split   *116*

Azikwelwa   *120*

A Case of Guilt   *128*

Caesar's Law   *139*

The Party   *151*

The Sacrifice   *163*

The Park   *172*

11.41 to Simonstown   *186*

A Clash of Colour   *195*

The Portable Radio

He gazed morosely at the shop windows as he slouched along the pavement, his feet kicking at small objects in front of him. He stopped at a large window displaying furniture in a modern bedroom setting.

He looked at the luxurious bed with its warm, downy blankets and imagined himself sinking into its yielding softness and covering himself with its warmth. He thought of his own bare room and reached out a hand to scratch himself where one of his bedfellows was having a late breakfast.

He could still hear the mean voice of his aunt when he told her of the insects sharing his bed. Her voice turned into a screech as she berated him.

'If it wasn't that you my sister's boy, the streets have you a long time ago. Here I getting old trying to run a respectable house and you not raising a hand to help me. Job after job the white people give you but work you don't. If you want your room clean, you do it!'

He grimaced as he relived the scene. He moved nearer to the window, his attention centred on the bed. It was built with a shelf that ran across the head to the floor on either side. The shelf was filled with books, and a portable radio took pride of place within reach of a reclining figure.

He leaned against the window and closed his eyes. It felt good. The warm blankets enfolded him and filled him with sensuous languor. He reached out a hand and switched on the radio on the shelf above his head, his fingers caressing the protruding knobs. He twisted one and moved from station to station like a bee in search of pollen, leaving a wake of news and music. Settling on one, he leaned back to enjoy the melody.

A rude voice threw him out of paradise. 'Look! Would you mind getting away from the window?'

The smug face and cleanliness of the white man made him wince inwardly. His own shirt was in such a condition that if he were to pass a laundry at less than five yards, the collar would drop off. He walked on, saddened.

'Anything we could offer you?' 'Shoes for the family?' 'Something for the house?' The voices of the shop assistants posted in front of their shops rang out for the benefit of the people passing. None of them had a word for him or spared him a glance as he walked past.

Sometimes he wished he had a steady job but he knew it could never be. Some time ago, a long time ago, he had had a job. But he could not stand it. The regular working hours were too confining. The large office filled with sunshine and white pretty girls in whose presence he always felt embarrassed. The sunshine he did not mind but the women in their freshly-starched frocks, bare-armed and smelling of lily of the valley, always made him acutely aware of them. Each time he passed or stood in front of them he broke into a cold sweat and could not resist looking at the curve of their breasts and the joggle of tightly-packed buttocks as they walked. He felt out of place among such an abundance of fresh femininity, and whenever he was sent out on an errand he would drop in at a bar along the way for a glass of wine. When the day ended he would be in a happy mood and smile at them when they bade him goodnight.

They sacked him when they discovered that, while drunk, he had forgotten to post a batch of important letters given earlier in the week. After that he lost job after job for the same reason. He drifted into casual work and the little he earned was spent on wine. He did not stop drinking despite his aunt's pleading and ranting.

He scarcely looked at the windows he passed. The trouble with his aunt was a thing of the past. Even his objectionable bedfellows were of no importance. His mind was filled with the portable radio he had seen. The richness of its colour, the gleaming plastic covering, the long shiny aerial, and the music he could get from it at will. Even the thought of wine was not strong enough to distract him from it.

His foot kicked against something heavy, the heel of his shoe dragging it along. The weight of the object shifted the last nail that held the heel secure. He stared with dismay at the heel which peeped back at him from the side of the shoe.

A small tobacco pouch was next to the heel.

His nerves tensed like a pointer spotting its quarry. He moved back to the wall and dragged the pouch with his foot. He scratched his calf nonchalantly. A few more scratches and the pouch was in his hand.

His fingers flowed over the unyielding surface. He was puzzled. The contents could not be tobacco; it was too bulky, and he could feel sharp edges. He undid the top while covering the pouch from observing eyes. The greenness of bank-notes wrapped around some object was revealed. Furtively he slipped the pouch into his pocket and walked away towards home.

He kept his hand in his pocket lest its contents disappear like some crazy dream. He was deliriously happy and felt like doing a dance on the pavement but, seeing a policeman on the corner, decided against it. The policeman might not understand his feelings of elation and arrest him for being drunk. He was not taking any chances with what he had in his pocket.

He ran the gauntlet of his aunt's sharp tongue as he made for his room. A glance showed that his aunt had made her usual search for concealed liquor. After making sure that the door was bolted he drew the pouch from his pocket, his fingers rubbing against it lovingly, and spilled the contents on the table. He unwrapped the bank-notes from the objects they covered and saw that they were four half-crowns.

There were eight five-pound notes. He arrayed them in a line, then changed the pattern. He made four piles and placed a half-crown on each pile. He lingered on the greenness. Forty pounds. A fortune.

A sound came from the doorway. He grabbed the money and shoved it into his pocket. He walked on tiptoe to the door and with one swift movement drew the bolt and swung it open.

His aunt was framed in the doorway like Cupid in the act of releasing an arrow.

'Why do you lock the door? If it's wine you bring into your room, you can just carry it out again. It's sick I am of the mess you make!'

'It's not wine I got,' he meekly replied.

'Remember what I say this morning!' With this last threat she waddled her way along the passage, the staircase protesting as she shifted her weight from foot to foot.

He searched his pockets for a stub of pencil, and on the back of a calendar that served also as a decoration, he worked out his fortune. He had more than enough to pay for the portable. He looked at himself in the mirror. He would have to buy something to wear first or else they might refuse to serve him. The white man with the smug face was not likely to let him pass the door without asking many questions.

His aunt was working in the kitchen; he could hear the banging of pots. Silently he crept down the stairs and out of the house.

He went to the second-hand shop where most of the neighbourhood bought their clothing. It also served as a clearing house for those with goods to sell.

He selected a white linen suit, a pair of canvas shoes and a pale blue shirt. He was drawn to a rattan cane on which hung a cheap panama hat. He could not resist the temptation and bought the lot, adding a blue and white candy-striped tie. He spotted a blanket on his way out, made a quick calculation, and bought it. With the generosity of the newly-rich, he threw the sixpence change to the boy helping in the shop.

His aunt spotted him before he could mount the stairs.

'Hey! What's that you got under your arms?' She eyed the bulky parcel suspiciously.

He took some money out of his pocket and gave

her a pound. 'I had some luck, Auntie. Buy yourself a present.'

She stood contemplating the money in her hand, and before she could speak, he was past her and climbing the steps to his room. She murmured something and put the money into the large pocket of the apron encasing her ample bosom.

He stood at the top of the stairs and called for hot water with which to shave. After some delay, his aunt pulled her bulk up the stairs. She slammed the container on the table with a baleful glare in his direction, splashing the water which she wiped off with the edge of her apron.

A hot bath and a shave later, he emerged resplendent in his new suit, panama hat dipped at a jaunty angle. With a twirl of his cane he walked down the stairs. His green-flecked teeth added colour to his brown face as he walked past his speechless aunt. 'I'll be back in a hour,' he said.

Each attendant vied for his attention as he walked past the shops in Waterkant Street.

The salesman did not recognise him when he entered the shop.

'What can I do for you, sir?'

He did not reply at once, savouring the servility of the salesman. He looked at a table and four padded chairs. Picking up a reading lamp, he watched the man hovering nearby. He turned towards him.

'I want to buy a portable radio.'

'Step this way, sir. I'll be glad to show you our latest models.' The salesman was like a cat confronted with a cup of cream. He was almost purring with pleasure.

He stood with affected boredom as if buying a radio set was a tiresome procedure.

The salesman flitted from set to set, twisting knobs, pulling out aerials, sending forth a blare of music with the twist of a wrist, praising one set for its colour scheme and another for its durability. He occupied himself with an imaginary speck of dust on his coat, carefully flicking it away with a large cotton handkerchief which he folded into a triangle and replaced in his breast pocket.

His choice was narrowed down to two sets. He had to choose between the glitter of one and the durability of the other. He held back. The portable with its shiny surface would surely raise him in the estimation of his aunt. On the other hand, the second set could be played by battery and when exhausted could be converted to electricity. The salesman was silent, hardly daring to breathe lest he disturb the fish nibbling at the hook. He took the set with the battery.

His aunt followed him into the room. Placing the portable on the table, he told her to close her eyes while he undid the wrapping. Reluctantly she complied with his request. He laughed as her face broke into pieces at the sight of the portable radio. He used all the technical terms he could remember as he explained to her how it worked and its advantages.

Work was forgotten while his aunt shared with him the hours of listening to the music. Even news reports were listened to with avid interest.

Dressed in his finery, he spent the days holding court in the bar on the corner and at night he would return swaying ever so slightly, and with the smell of wine on his breath. His aunt overlooked it all, and a plate of hot food awaited him each night.

In the dim glow of his room, and covered by the extra warmth of his new blanket, he would ease back, stroking the soft surface of the blanket while the music flowed over him in waves of contentment.

His aunt tolerated him even when his drinking bouts became more frequent and lasted longer, until finally he had no more money left.

The panama hat and the rattan cane were the first to go. It brought him enough to buy a bottle of wine. He held on to the suit as long as he could but his thirst was too strong. The second-hand dealer stood with a complacent air as he handed over the money.

He was too dispirited to argue and walked listlessly from the store. Around his neck was the candy-coloured tie curling at the edges but still making a brave attempt to strike a gay note, making him look like a discarded Christmas tree. His canvas shoes completed the picture, adding a smell of their own.

He walked home with the two bottles of wine ignoring the pleas from his former courtiers.

He put the two bottles down on the table and switched on the portable. The indicator showed no bright gleam. He tried it again with the same result. Then it dawned on him that the electricity was cut off. He turned a knob at the back of the portable and converted it to battery. The indicator jumped to life when he switched it on and music rushed forth.

His aunt entered the room and glared at him. The wine had removed his fear of her. 'You forget about the batteries.' His voice ended in a giggle. She slammed the door.

He took off his shoes and fell back on the bed with a bottle near at hand.

A roar of music woke him the next morning. His throat was dry. Next to the bed stood the remaining bottle which he opened and held up, the wine trickling from the side of his mouth.

The continuous playing soon drained the batteries and he spent miserable days cooped up in his room.

Through the window he could see the time on the foundry clock. It would be a good four hours before his aunt would switch on the lights. He stretched himself out on the bed and tried to sleep.

The light streaming from beneath the door when he awoke told him that it was time to switch on the portable.

He fiddled around with the dial, trying each waveband in turn. He tuned into stations he never knew existed.

Brazil called with the throb of drums pounding out a South American rhythm that jerked his body alive. Mexico contributed a fiesta, bringing to mind a vision of pretty señoritas and gay caballeros strumming guitars and dancing a fandango. The plaintive wail of a clarinet moaning the 'Birth of the Blues' welcomed him to the U.S.

He turned it on to its full volume, the music flooding his room and spilling out into the passage, rolling downstairs until it filled the house.

The music was a drug and it soothed him.

It was suddenly snatched away in the midst of its healing as the lights went off in the passage. He looked at the portable and then grabbed it by its sides and shook it violently. From outside the door his aunt called him. 'See how you like it. I had enough of you. I turn off the light and tomorrow you clear out and take that damn box of noise with you.' Then she laughed. Louder, ever louder, until it seemed that the now silent portable had somehow been transplanted inside her. 'Hee-hee, haw-haw,' her laughter lashed, sending him cringing beneath the blankets with his fingers pressed into his ears. 'Hee-hee, haw-haw,' it rumbled around him. He flung the blankets aside and grabbed the portable, raised it overhead and smashed it against the wall. 'Hee-hee, haw-haw, ho-ho.' It was still present, stronger, louder, a dynamo of diabolical merriment. 'Hee-hee, haw-haw, ho-ho-ho.' The peals of laughter made his body writhe.

Eyes glazed, he took hold of the empty bottle, smashed the top on the edge of the table, and crept quietly from the room to silence the 'hee-hee, haw-haw, ho-ho-ho' that threatened to tear him to shreds.

Incident

With a muted clickety-clack the train passed under the bridge and came to a halt in the station after a series of convulsive jerks that shook him awake. From behind the misted panes he squinted at the familiar billboard with the poster depicting a white couple clad in bathing costumes and enjoying a can of beer on a beach he could never share. The chill was like death met head-on and he hesitated before stepping out from the warmth of the coach to the cold of the platform. Behind him, head poked out through a window, a ticket examiner hurried the crowd reluctant to leave the third-class carriage. Turtle-like, he pulled his neck deeper into his coat collar and hurried towards the subway.

One more day done, or rather, one more night, he told himself as he walked down the street away from the station. A dog howled at his appearance. The howl was taken up by other dogs farther on marking his progress. He peered at the sky piled with dirty, grey clouds poised as if to smash against each other and drench the earth below. I only hope I get home before they let go.

Ahead of him, a block away, scurried one of his

fellow-passengers on the twenty-minutes-after-mid-
night from Cape Town to Southfield. I bet he's running to get next to his woman in bed. He smiled at
the thought of Letty, blanket-covered and flushed
with sleep. Behind him — he could hear them — came
the band who worked as casual hands at the fishing
company in the harbour, the wind carrying their
words; jeers, jokes and laughter. The wind also carried
the smell of the sea mixed with the blood of thousands
of gutted fish impregnated in their clothes.

Underneath a lamppost, in front of him, stood his
impatient fellow-passenger, halted by two over-
coated figures. Even without the light shining on
them he would have known they were policemen. He
walked towards them, speculating on the cause of the
stoppage. Perhaps he was stopped because of the bag
he was carrying. His mind went back to the number
of times, in town, on the way to the station, he had
been stopped by them. The insolent 'Hey, come here'
from a snot-nosed, uniformed eighteen-year-old, and
the hold-back-your-anger voice tonelessly replying to
the inane questions. Uneasiness, mixed with anger,
filled him. The man was released when he was abreast
of them.

He stood, surprised at what to him was an absurd
question to be asked.

Where would I be going, if not home, in weather
like this, and at this time of the morning?

He stared at the white policeman who had spoken,
then shifted his gaze to the face of the other policeman. The brown face underneath the khaki helmet
was withdrawn as if its presence was coincidental and
had no relationship to the scene.

'Home.'

'What's in the bag?'

He shook the suspect bag. A few drops of rain trickled past his ear and down his neck. He shivered. I'm for it.

'A towel, wash cloth, piece of soap, and a loaf of bread.' He smiled. Now, I suppose he's going to ask me where I got the bread from.

The policeman's next question was even more surprising, bordering on the ridiculous.

'What have you got hidden under your arm?'

The object could be seen clearly.

Raindrops falling on his face assured him that he was not dreaming.

'Newspaper and book.'

'Ahh. Let me see?'

'I've only the one paper,' he said, holding on to one end, 'and I haven't read it yet.'

'Who the hell wants your damn paper!' the policeman snapped in aggrieved tones.

He was puzzled.

If it's not the paper then what does he want?

'Come'n, away with you to the charge office!' To the other policeman. 'You see to that loudmouth bunch of Hotnots coming down the road.'

He opened his mouth to say that they were from the harbour but changed his mind. A man who had to be told what was in open sight could not be relied upon to trust his sense of smell.

Bewilderment clouded his head as he followed along to the charge office. He could hear them guying the coloured policeman. 'Hey, you guys. Here's the law.' 'Hello, my black boss.' The last one evoking loud laughter.

'Is Detective-Sergeant Williams on duty?' he asked, voice filled with a confidence he did not share. He had heard of what sometimes happened in charge offices at night. I'm not going to get beaten up if I can help it. I've met Williams once but there's nothing wrong in letting this one know that I also know people in the force.

'I trust Williams just as much as I trust the rest of you swart volk!'

He had a wild desire to turn about and wrench the door open as it swung shut, and dash down the street, but fear of what would follow dampened his desire.

An African constable lounged at the counter, one finger exploring the cavity of a wide nostril. Behind the counter was a coloured sergeant seated at a desk laboriously typing out a report. In front of a heater, in a chair, sprawled another sergeant — white. On the wall, facing the counter, was a picture of the Minister of Justice, a benevolent smile on his face. The trio favoured them with a brief glance, turning each to his activity.

'Give me that book you were hiding under your arm.'

He was no longer amazed at what was asked of him.

The book was slammed down on the counter.

'Where did you get this book from?'

'From the library.'

'Which library?'

'Kewtown branch. It's stamped on the back.'

The policeman swished through the pages, found the stamp imprint and disappointedly returned to the front.

The coloured sergeant looked at them, two fingers poised over the keyboard. He was not sure of the message — There's nothing I can do — or was it — Don't blame me.

The policeman seemed to have run out of questions and was fluttering the pages without bothering to read the print.

The African constable, having exhausted the possibilities of his nostrils, disappeared down a corridor, the examination promising nothing of interest.

'What are you doing with this book?'

He did not know whether he should laugh. Then he nervously asked himself: Hell, don't tell me this book has been banned since I last checked a newspaper?

Before he could reply ('Since when is it a crime to read a book?'), the white sergeant, without changing his position, spoke.

'Away with you!' And he stomped his way down a corridor leading to the depths of the police station.

Leaving the charge office, he remembered that somewhere, in some book he had read, a character had said: 'The law is an ass!' He disagreed. There's nothing wrong with the law itself. The trouble is that there are too many donkeys in its employ.

He left the doubtful shelter of the charge office and walked into a curtain of rain. Before he had reached the corner his coat moulded his back. He laughed out loud as he walked in the rain, the offending book pressed to his heart and the newspaper spread over his head and shoulders, his bag smacking against his knees.

The Man Who Was Too Small

He made a grotesque figure as he walked. The huge trunk swayed from side to side supported by short, thin, bandy legs. His oversized head, perched on top of his stalky neck, trembled perilously with each step. The face was turned into a caricature by the huge mound of flesh serving as a nose and the tiny ears stuck on each side of the head; thick lips uncurled into a smile that revealed teeth like the keys of an old piano. His eyes were as soft and innocent of guile as those of a dove.

A baby, unattended, played with a ball of wool on the stoep of a ramshackle double-storey house. A kitten darted through the doorway and joined the game. The kitten jabbed a paw and hooked the ball. The baby grabbed the kitten's ear and the kitten retaliated with a swift slash. The baby's cry brought its mother on the scene. She retrieved the ball of wool and pitched the kitten into the street where it let out a piteous wail. This scene drew a responding chuckle from the baby.

The man turned the corner and walked into a line of drunken men. He scuttled back before they could form a circle trapping him, and stood pressed against the wall.

Their drunken taunts battered him and he raised short, ineffective arms in defence, tears of impotence wetting his breasts.

'Dwarf!' 'Tokoloshe!' 'Short-arse!'

Each word inflicted pain sharper than a blow. One of the tormentors lurched forward, his hand outstretched in a taunt. He pulled at the hand in front of his face and sank his teeth into it. His victim yelped with pain and stared stupidly at the pattern of tooth marks, the edges dripping blood. Their attention distracted, he moved with a duck-like gait to the shelter of a stoep on the other side of the street.

Their ranting attracted a small crowd of spectators who joined in the derisive laughter.

He slid off the stoep and continued his walk, ignoring the cackle mocking his footsteps.

They're all the same. Young and old. And the women are worse than the men. The men, when drunk, will jeer at you, and, at times, one might strike you, but most of the time they leave you alone. But not women! Minds like cesspools, they befoul me with their filth. I hate them, all of them, every breast-feeding bitch! I hate them! He repeated his hatred to himself over and over until it became a litany from which he could draw comfort, yet knowing that it would be as comfortless as a hair-shirt and that he would never give up secretly hoping that one day he might find a woman who would look at him without revulsion.

When completely alone, he would resort to a dream which for the moment brought him peace and forgetfulness. He was in a land where everyone was afflicted. There were those who were lame; those who were blind; those who had humps on their backs; and there were those like himself. The blind were comforted by the lame and the mis-shapen were kind to him, and in their eyes shone love and no one was unwanted.

His face was lit by a smile and his eyes sparkled with the joy of his thoughts. The drab street was transformed. The pails of garbage at doorways, the gutters running with scum, the drunk sleeping off his carousing, the small boy eating an orange peel streaked with dirt — all of it he did not see.

He could hardly contain himself as he walked. His mind lingered lovingly on the fantasy he wove.

A flood of obscenities spilled from his mouth and was answered by the laughter of his tormentors.

His rage had drained his energy and he rested on the stoep of a tenement house. The combined smell of stale cooking, the stench from slime-filled gutters, and over-spilling pails of garbage did not seem to affect him.

A window opened above his head and an old crone croaked in a harsh voice, 'What are you doing sitting there? Get away from the door before you bring bad luck. Or is it a woman you're wanting? You, whose very face dries the milk in their breasts!'

A throaty cackle followed her speech, then she leaned over the window-sill and spat. The spittle fell next to him and a few drops touched his hand. Her words hurt. Insults and abuse he considered his lot, but each fresh assault caught him unprepared. Often, he had watched a woman, unaware of him, busy at some task, or nursing a baby at her breast, and experienced a longing which he knew could never be fulfilled. Invariably, they would turn their faces at his approach, even screaming their terror before he could tell them that he meant no harm. He would hurry away with the shame of his deformity.

He glared at the old woman, and from the pit of hatred inside him drew an answer. 'You dirty old bitch who has long forgotten what it is to be a woman, and who is bad luck itself, how could you know what I'm doing here? Maybe you hope it's you I want. You, who not even the devil wants. Why don't you get yourself to the grave?'

'I've had more men than you'll ever have women. And all of them were men and not a piece of man like yourself, half-penny!'

He was in a meadow. Seated next to him was a woman. He could not determine her age. She reached out a hand and took hold of his and smiled at him when he raised his head to meet her eyes. Behind them, in a tree, a bird was serenading the sun, and the flowers opened their petals in homage to its song. Two children played at their feet — a boy and a girl — and he knew that he had fathered them. The girl turned from play and called the woman mother. She smiled at the child and squeezed his hand . . . . His happiness crowded out all other feelings.

The blare of a lorry's hooter rocketed him back to reality. He just had enough time to hop on to the pavement as the lorry roared past, the curses of the driver scorching the air.

Try as he would, he could not reweave the fantasy. The pattern was destroyed by the interruption.

He entered a narrow house. In a back room sat three women.

'Hello,' he grunted with downcast eyes.

'It's old half-jack!' one exclaimed. Another said: 'Hello, yourself, small-shit!' He suffered their scorn in silence, then he addressed the third woman who did not bother to look at him.

'Could I have a bottle, please?' he asked diffidently.

She looked up from her sewing and said, 'It's two bottles you're down for.' He nodded his head in agreement. 'Maria, give him one.'

One of the women got up from the worn-out couch, its springs protesting as she moved, and shifted a medicine chest placed in a corner of the room. She pressed her foot on a floorboard which slid aside to reveal seven bottles of wine. She removed one and wiped off the dust with the hem of her skirt before handing it to him.

He filled a glass which he sipped while watching the women. The one who was sewing finished her task and left the room. The other two, as if freed from restraint, moved nearer to him.

Maria placed two glasses in front of him. 'How about it? Are you going to finish it by yourself?' Her companion eyed the bottle.

He filled their glasses. They drained the wine in one long swallow and sat waiting. He hurriedly sipped what remained in his glass. He refilled the glasses, emptying the bottle.

The wine filled him with a comforting warmth, stilling his caution in dealing with them.

'Maria,' he said, 'ask her if I could get another one.'

Maria cast a sly look at her friend. 'Why not two? She trusts you. Everybody knows you always square your debts.' Then she added, 'Besides, with two bottles we could have nice times. Just the three of us.'

She left the room before he could say a word.

The procedure with the medicine chest was repeated on her return.

She opened a bottle, put it to her mouth and swallowed deeply before handing it to him.

'That's the stuff,' she said.

Now that there was more wine inside him, the women seemed to have changed. They seemed not much different from women whose children he had fathered in his fantasy. He held Maria's arm and stroked it when she reached for her glass. She allowed his caresses and transferred the glass to the other hand. She smiled as she drank and he became bolder. The other woman noticed the by-play.

'Don't you think that I'm as pretty as Maria?' she asked, her voice soft and pleading. 'Come on, make love to me.'

She changed her position so that he sat between them.

They squealed their delight when his fumbling hand touched a breast, all the time draining their glasses until, the wine at an end and his desire at its height, they pushed him away and pummelled his body as he lay sprawled across the couch.

'That's for touching me with your dirty little paws!' ...'You think I'd let you, an animal, have me?' they screamed as they struck him.

He dropped to the floor and crawled underneath the table. They jabbed their shoes in his ribs as he lay cowering. 'Bitches! Bitches!' he drunkenly mumbled.

'Leave him alone!'

Their kicking ceased.

'He started it,' Maria snarled. 'He gave us wine, and now he wants us to lay with him!'

A hand touched his shoulder but he was past caring and let himself drift away.

He was alone when he awoke. He left the house without anyone seeing him leave. His humiliation was heavy upon him. His hatred was mixed with self-pity.

I'll make them suffer like I'm suffering. Why am I

cursed like this? If only I were big like other people. They would come running after me then, but I wouldn't touch them. Stinking whores!

He walked aimlessly, not wanting to go back to the cold, cheerless shack in the backyard where he lived on his own.

He found himself in front of the billiard saloon. In the front room the card players were absorbed in their game. He moved to the hall at the end of the passage.

Two men were angled across the billiard table and a third acted as marker. A sharp click-clack at intervals was the only sound. At the end of play the marker called: 'Seven for Spot, making the score 84 to 79. Spot leading.'

The two players paused, resting on their cues, then turned towards him, seeking a diversion to end the boredom of the game. It had gone on for hours, the three of them changing partners at the completion of each frame.

'Come on, Tiny. Give me a game,' one of the players said. 'Show them what they still got to learn.' Turning to the others, he continued: 'Tiny doesn't even need a cue. He uses his nose to pot them. Show us how you do it, Tiny.'

Before he could move he was hoisted into the air, his arms pinned to his sides, and lowered to the table. His forehead touched the soft felt. They roared their merriment as his nose bumped a ball, sending it rolling. 'Score a cannon off the black.'

He squirmed feebly as he was pushed along the table. His body went limp. When he made no response to the agony inflicted upon him, he was dropped on to the floor. He sat there rubbing his nose, their jeers striking him like blows.

They resumed their game.

The well of hatred inside him overflowed. He bathed in its waters, soaking himself, filling every pore. Behind his closed eyelids his eyes were two whirlpools dragging them down into the well and drowning them.

Their boredom became too much for them. A wild shot which sent the balls cannoning across the table ended the game.

The two players left the hall for the card room, not bothering to look at him seated on the floor. The marker cleared the table of balls and spread himself on top of it.

He sat brooding on the floor and the marker's snores roused him to action.

'I'll show you,' he muttered. 'Treat me like shit!'

He had no idea what he was going to do. His eyes swept the room. The billiard cue? No, it was too unwieldy. The balls? Yes! He could do a lot of damage with a ball slammed into an unsuspecting face. He pushed the chair against the table and struggled on top of it.

He stood erect, his foot on the jacket of the sleeper. Just then his foot felt an object in the pocket. He stooped and removed it. He looked at the razor in his hand. He opened it. The edge was filed to a gleaming sharpness.

Why not? They won't ever laugh at me again. He pressed a finger along the edge of the razor. The skin parted. A red ribbon decorated it.

He sank to his knees. He looked at the neck in front of him, the tendons standing out, the beating pulse. He bent forward. Placed blade against flesh. Pressed and pulled towards him. The skin parted like sliced fruit, displaying a pulpy mess bathed in bloody juice. Halfway across the eyes bulged open in uncomprehending horror and then a low gurgle was heard as he reached the other side. The green felt greedily lapped up the rich, red blood. He placed the now crimson razor on the chest of the corpse and inspected his handiwork. He knew what he was going to do next but he was in no hurry. He wiped his hands on the felt, hung from the side of the table and let go.

He was not disturbed by the movements of the card players in front. He moved to the yard. The toilet was in a corner. He locked the door.

Monkey-like he scrambled up the pipe and perched on top of the cistern. The chain was cool around his neck. He secured it with a length of twine he had in his pocket. He tugged. It held. Then he sat waiting. Without an effort he found himself back in the land of fantasy.

The two children had garlanded him with flowers and the woman gazed at him with laughing eyes and did not see his deformity. The afflicted sat around feasting and the lame danced to music provided by the blind. His happiness overwhelmed him. 'Jesus Christ! Look at his throat,' someone screamed. Then he jumped to meet those who loved him.

Whites Only

His happy mood was swamped by a feeling of numbness and his breath came in short gasps as he walked past the long line of railway coaches marked 'Whites Only'. A violent throbbing started inside his head and the rows of white faces he passed became a blur which intensified his nausea and increased the tempo of the throbbing inside his head.

White bastards! They must have everything reserved for them.

They must always be first in line for every good thing. Even when a black man does the same job, the white bastard gets double the pay.

His impotence burst out in a thick splash of spittle against the side of the coach he was passing. The woman seated at the window turned her face with a grimace of disgust at his action. He stopped, deliberately placed a finger at the side of his nose, and ejected a stream of snot. He repeated the action through his other nostril and smeared his hand on the side of the coach before walking on. He smiled as the window closed, the jerky rattle showing the anger of the woman.

His mood was further dampened by the line of

Africans shovelling stones between the twin steel tracks. A well-built white man was at their head, open neck, arms and face baked a dull red by the sun's rays. He stood hands-on-hips, in his mouth a whistle which he blew at the sound of the approaching train. The Africans sank on their haunches as the train slithered to a halt next to them. The whites seated in the coaches let their eyes drift over them, then beyond them to the people on the platform.

He returned their stare with an anger which left them untouched as they swept their gaze past him.

Get up from your knees and put down your tools, he silently screamed at the kneeling row of black men. You are free men! They spoke to each other in their tongue, blissfully ignorant of his message, and laughed loudly, showing teeth planted in scarlet gums.

He turned away in disgust and joined the queue at the ticket-box, glaring resentfully at the 'non-white' metal plate fixed above the window. He paused as long as he dared when it was his turn to be served.

'Third class return to Cape Town, please.' Voice soft and servile. He searched all his pockets for the money, all the time watching the growing annoyance of the white clerk, producing it just before the clerk's annoyance reached boiling point. 'Thank you.' Mockery in his voice as he took the ticket flung at him.

His ruse filled him with elation. He stood on the platform scorning the seats allocated to blacks, inwardly sneering at those seated. His restlessness made him irritable and his glance shifted from object to object. His nails worried a scab on the back of his right hand.

He walked to the other end of the platform. He did not want anything in particular but the impulse was irresistible when he saw the white woman seated in the partitioned news-stand. He shaped his face into one of innocence and asked for a copy of *Die Burger*. As she handed it to him, he said: 'What has the great white father in store for us today?' She felt the ridicule behind his words and a deep flush stained her cheeks. He did not bother to read the paper and as he walked he tore it into long strips which he stuffed into a waste-bin attached to a pole.

An elderly woman sat reading a paper. The letters were stark against the white surface. 'White Students Protest Against Black Student Deprived Of Passport'. She looked at him from behind her glasses, eyes blinking solemnly. 'The white people are not all bad. It's only the Boere,' she said. He smiled at her.

Yes, they're not all bad. They're only full of deceit. At the office they are very nice to me. The typist has an ever-bright smile for me, and the men with a breezy 'good morning' hide the effort it costs them to conceal their resentment as I join them, doing the same clerical work. At lunchtime they rush from the office as if to be free of my presence, if only for an hour. And the indignity of being told by the caretaker that I'm not to use the toilet reserved for whites, that I'm to use the toilet hidden in the yard and used by the other dark-skinned workers. The gleaming toilet with its mirrored walls is only to be used by those with white skins. And, once, when I was foolish enough to attend the Christmas Eve party held in the office each year, I saw that the typist was careful always to serve me in the same glass which she kept on one side of the tray, all the while smiling sweetly at me. And when the others danced with her in turn, I had to pretend that I wasn't there. Yes, and all the good work done for the poor, suffering blacks, and always receiving lots of space in the papers for their good deeds.

'Yes,' he said, 'the white people are very good to us. That's why we have *apartheid,* so that we can develop along our own lines. And, as the great white father has promised us, we'll also have our state within a state. Only he didn't make it quite clear when it will come off.'

She looked at him, puzzled.

That should wake you up, he silently added, his eyes still smiling at her.

The arrival of the train brought a rush as the doors slid open and people tumbled out, pushing aside those striving for admittance. Beside the coach, apart from the bustle, stood a ticket examiner who bawled in a loud voice, 'Alle stasies na Kaapstad — All stations to Cape Town.'

He stopped to help a pregnant woman with two children and settled opposite them.

'Kaartjies asseblief — Tickets, please.' The ticket examiner announced his presence.

The syllables grated on his ear. The authority-filled voice raised his bile. He concentrated his attention on the small girl on the opposite seat. She had a rag doll on her lap and was telling her brother that it had wet its clothes. She poked a reproving finger in the doll's face, bending it backwards. The doll replied with a musical 'ma'.

The examiner filled the space between them and he thrust out his ticket without looking at the outstretched hand.

The examiner barked at an African who looked bewilderedly in his pockets and produced two tickets, both wrong ones. The ticket examiner snorted his annoyance and plucked the ticket from the African's breast pocket where it peeped out. He punched the ticket and tossed it into the African's lap. As he turned, he said, 'Kaffirs are forever stupid!'

He winced as if the humiliation had been his and looked at the African who appeared already to have forgotten the incident, puffing unconcernedly at his pipe.

As they pulled in to Cape Town station, he opened the door and jumped out without waiting for the train to stop, ignoring the examiner's warning.

Everywhere he looked was evidence of the white man's power. The station filled with workers supervised by white foremen. A coloured policeman standing meekly to attention while speaking to a white policeman of the same rank. His eyes lit up with pride at the sight of a coloured traffic constable moving on a car driven by a white, but when he entered the huge department store across from the station, his pride fizzled out before the many counters and the white attendants behind them. He walked to the fruit juice stand.

The two attendants continued their conversation. He listened as they relived the previous evening. 'And was I surprised when I answered the door and found him standing there with a box of chocolates. You could've knocked me down with a feather but I made as if nothing had happened, and asked him what he wanted.' 'And what did he say?' That's right. Keep it up. I don't exist. He looked at their faces — masks ineptly made up. Powder laid in uneven layers and the lipstick smeared beyond the borders of their lips, staining the teeth. A white couple joined him and the girls reluctantly broke off their conversation to turn to them with painful smiles.

He took the escalator down to the self-service basement and from a pile of baskets took one. He helped himself from the stacked shelves. Why can't they arrange everything like this? No attendants who think they're doing you a favour when they serve you. He did not mind the slight delay at the cash-desk. He maintained his feeling of well-being when a stout white woman, pudgy fingers lined with rings, pushed past him.

Outside, the air was heavy with the fragrance of flowers. His senses enjoyed the smell and sight of flowers sprouting from wide, steel buckets but his enjoyment was marred by the sellers who called out, 'Master! Merrum! Pretty roses, carnations. Very cheap, master!' He despised their servility and yet envied the beauty they presented as they sat in rows with their flower-filled buckets in front of them. The women wore broad-brimmed straw hats and gaily-printed aprons. Heavy earrings dangled from their ears. The men were busy with their hands, strapping bundles of heaped flowers. The chatter of the children was the chirping of birds as they darted between the feet of passing people.

He gave no heed to their cries and walked slowly, looking at the faces of the sellers. He stopped in front of an old woman who sat with quiet dignity, hands folded across her stomach. This is the one. He selected a bunch from the blaze of colour in her bucket and paid more than the price quoted. She smiled her thanks.

A young girl, breasts firm and face beautiful, dipped in front of a white couple and held her offering aloft for their scrutiny. He was filled with sadness. He knew that his anger could not right anything. Even if he were to rush to the side of the girl and drag her to her feet. If he were to tell them that all men are equal, no matter what their tasks, they would only look at him with the vacant air of cattle, and some, sensing a loss of business in his talk, would turn against him. He stood to one side, out of the way of the crowd, absorbing a scene filled with movement and colour.

One more thing, he told himself, then I'm free to leave Cape Town with all its signs of white domination.

He entered the lobby of the post office and walked past the three telephone booths marked 'white' and the adjoining two marked 'non-white'.

A white man had his hand on the door of one of the 'non-white' booths when his companion jokingly said, 'Since when are you black?' The white man looked at the metal sign above the phone booth and replied, 'It's a good thing you saw it or else I would've placed a receiver used by a Kaffir next to my ear.'

He glared at them, their backs to him, his hatred naked on his face.

The main hall had its counters marked off for white and non-white. Near the door leading to the street was the counter where he had to get his radio licence. He joined the queue.

The familiar irritation stirred in his breast. Must it always be like this? Even when we have to pay them they make us wait, as if our money were nothing.

He spat between his feet, for once unconcerned about the worker who swept the hall with wide sweeps of his broom, whistling while he worked.

A woman was involved in an argument with the clerk at the counter. In an effort to rid himself of her, the clerk briskly called out to the next in line but the woman refused to give up her place.

'I won't move,' she said. 'I want my money. It's ours. Every week my man come and bring it to you to mark in the book — and now we want it, you can't come and tell me that I can't get it!'

That's right, lady. You tell him. Don't let them push you around. He stood up straighter.

The clerk's voice registered his resignation. 'Listen. Take this form home and get your husband to sign it.'

The woman's victory sparked him, and as she walked away, he winked at her.

One of the uniformed attendants approached the queue and checked as to who had to pay radio licences. Four people left the queue and he joined them as they walked to the other side of the hall where whites were served.

The young girl behind the counter looked at them and sniffed. After serving three whites she turned to them. Her relief was evident when a white youth approached the counter. He watched her expression change when she had to turn to them once more, and the twitch of revulsion her hand gave as it accidentally touched a black hand when the money was passed over.

Her agitation increased as she continued to serve them. She slid off her high stool when there was only one more to be served before him, and disappeared behind a partition screening her from the public.

The queue lengthened as more whites came, and a man with a military bearing asked the attendant what had happened to the girl.

The attendant walked to the front of the queue and called out, 'Miss van Tonder?' After a delay, the girl appeared with a handkerchief clasped to her eyes.

'What's the matter, Miss van Tonder? Are you ill?' The attendant had to repeat his question before the girl replied.

'I've got a big pile of cheques to sort and I've got to serve as well, and you keep sending them to me!'

The words came out in a torrent and she pointed a finger at the coloured men.

He looked at the whites. Some of them avoided his eyes, their gaze fixed on some object on the far side of the hall. A youth sniggered. The attendant addressed them in an apologetic tone. 'Would you please go to the other side of the hall and I'll get someone else to serve you.' He glanced at his companion, who left the counter without a protest.

He looked at the lines of whites, at the apologetic attendant, and the girl behind the counter who looked triumphantly at the retreating back of his companion.

The hall, the girl, the attendant, everybody and everything else disappeared in the anger that consumed him. His body was on fire and he had to blink hard to keep the tears back. He could not think coherently. His mind was filled with obscenities which were repeated over and over until it became a blank screen with the obscenities flashing on it in multicoloured letters. The struggle to clear his mind set his body atremble. He stared at their white faces. To free the words from his mind and watch the reaction: he did not dare to do it.

Impotence flooded him and he could only curse himself silently. Oh, you spineless son-of-a-bitch! Why don't you throw the money in her face? It's so simple. All you have to do is raise your hand, open it, and let fly. Are you going to prove that she's right, that because your skin isn't white, you cannot be called a man? The fuse in his mind blew and the screen was blank.

'Come along, please,' the attendant said and he meekly followed, his body strangely dead and heavy, back to the growing queue on the other side of the hall.

Mistaken Identity

Friday night, and the district was filled with people glad that the working week was over. They showed their appreciation in many ways, one of which was a priority with most of the working males, not forgetting those for whom work was anathema. Some had begun earlier than others, Robbie Stevens one of the first among them. He was pleasantly drunk and as he stood rocking on his heels, he regarded the world with an abundance of goodwill which he otherwise would not have accorded it.

His world, for the moment, consisted of a little slum street, with cluttered houses, one leaning against the other and all in need of paint to conceal brick-blemished plaster, evidence of the onslaught of winter's rain. Two of his world's inhabitants approached him: a little boy and a big dog. The boy stuck out his tongue when he spoke to him and the dog pissed on his trousers in passing. He shrugged his shoulders philosophically at them, his goodwill undiminished.

'Where is the moon tonight?' he sang, with a high and unmelodic voice.

A hawker on his way home, pushing a barrow with the remains of his sales, stopped beside him.

'How about a dop?' asked the hawker in a hopeful tone.

Robbie Stevens shook his head regretfully.

'Sorry, pellie. Die joep is op.'

'Take some fruit home for the old lady and the kids. You can have them for cheap. Delicious bananas. Six for a bob. Little bit bruise but never you mind. Try my method if you got a problem with the old lady. It's always good with bananas.'

More in sympathy than need, he exchanged cash for bananas, and the hawker moved on with his barrow.

He peeled a banana, placed it in his mouth and swallowed it with gusto. His sleeve was used as a handkerchief and he continued his lament for a love lost.

'Baby, I miss you.' He stilled his lament at the approach of two old women. They were dressed in black from top to toe. Their heads were adorned with black straw hats on which artificial flowers served as decoration. They wore low-heeled shoes, the fronts pointed. The V of their dresses sheltered discreetly under scarves of blue, pinned down by cameo brooches the size of a dove's egg.

'Good evening, ladies. What's going on?' he asked, head held at a slant.

They continued their walk without consenting to answer, leaving behind an odour of lavender mixed with a trace of peppermint.

'That's not nice, ladies,' he said reproachfully. 'And I was going to offer you some bananas.'

They crossed the street and stopped outside a door, paused for an instant to adjust their clothing, and then entered after knocking lightly. Robbie Stevens heard the sound of voices raised in song before the door closed behind them. The melody sounded familiar in some way. It was a hymn. His memory deceived him and the words tumbled out in incorrect order as he tried to give shape to it.

He swayed across the road as if the old women had rerouted his destination. He knocked longer and louder than he intended. The door swung open and he stood surprised, with fist suspended.

'Yes, yes. What do you want?'

He thrust a banana at the woman who had opened the door and forced his way past her.

Voices flowed from the room nearest the door. The sound reached him via a group packing the passage which led to the rear of the house. From the kitchen came the faint echo of a hymn.

He pressed himself forward. He could see, above the heads of those in front of him, a plain brown coffin with brass handles that glittered in the lamplight.

Those he had elbowed aside looked at him askance, taking in his dishevelled clothes — shirt torn and jacket coated with vomit; his rumpled hair; his blood-shot eyes, the slackness of his thick, coffee-coloured lips, their insides pink as the shell of a snail.

The waters and the blood
Flow from you riven side.

It was a mixed assembly of voices — firm basses, quivering sopranos, and youthful tenors in support.

The hymn ended and he moved forward to peer into the coffin.

The body — with the exception of the face and the upper part of the chest on which the hands lay clasped — was covered with a blanket of flowers. The head was shorn of hair and beneath the hairline, if there had been one, were two dark eyebrows raised as if encouraging him to react, and which seemed as if at any moment they would quiver in recognition.

'Just think, you too, old pellie! We can do what we like but we cannot escape from it, and in the end it will get us all!'

He grunted, took out a shilling from his pocket and dropped it in a saucer placed there for that purpose. He knocked over the saucer as he turned around and the money clattered to the floor.

'Daar's nou kak!' he said, and sank down on his haunches to salvage the strewn coins. He bumped into the table on which the coffin rested when he raised himself. The coffin shifted alarmingly and people hurried from their chairs to support it. He looked at them confusedly as they bustled around him.

'Who is he?' 'Where does he come from?' 'What is he doing here?' Noisily they jostled him towards the door.

The two old women, from their places in the corner, regarded the scene without changing expression, jaws still working industriously — the only sign that they were interested.

'I know him,' Robbie Stevens began. Tears ran down his cheeks, his emotional outburst evoking more disgust. He was pushed hurriedly into the passage away from the mourners, who sat with dignity and respect regained.

He tried again. 'But you don't understand.'

No one responded. He tottered down the passage towards the kitchen when the backs turned on him blocked off his appeal for understanding.

Two youths who had been entertained by his performance waited until he was even with them, then one thrust out a leg while the other shoved him in the small of his back, sending him sprawling into the

kitchen. With a supressed laugh they sought protection in the crowd around the door of the room containing the coffin.

Five people — four small girls and an old woman
— were in the kitchen. The girls went into spasms of
giggles at his unconventional entry into the kitchen,
their laughter soon stifled by a sharp glance from the
old woman.

He got up off his knees and sat on a low stool with
his back resting against the wall and his feet comfortably stretched.

The kitchen table seemed to be a garden of flowers.
Heaps of greenery lay at their feet. The scent of flowers
was not quite strong enough to dispel the traces of
past suppers, in which fried fish and cabbage had
predominated.

Voices were raised in a hymn and he sought comfort
from it. He sat with a bemused smile on his face as he
observed the old woman's delicate fingers transform a
simple wooden cross into a green symbol of grief.

He reflected upon the many wakes he had attended,
and on the body occupying the coffin inside. The
many friends, dead. And always the wakes, and the
room, the room sometimes one flight up, or on the
ground floor, and sometimes in the yard, the room
where they always met to talk about the dead one.
And always the bottles of wine, consumed while they
talked.

Death, for him, was nothing frightening. It was as
inevitable as a crowded bar on a public holiday. He
laughed aloud and the old woman raked him with a
poisonous glance while at the same time she held the
four girls in check to prevent a fresh outburst of
hilarity.

He recalled the last funeral he had attended. He

had not been altogether sober and had to borrow a tie. To follow a coffin to the grave without wearing a tie was to him as reprehensible as refusing to share wine with another drinker.

He had first offered condolence to the bereaved relatives before going to the room where those who came to mourn, mourned with libations. He took his place, not in any of the cars reserved for the chief mourners, but in a hired bus when the coffin was transferred to the hearse. He followed the familiar route to the cemetery from a window on the upper deck.

They had gone along the red gravel path with small pebbles grinding under their feet; passed the many graves, some sunken, others new mounds of earth, some with crosses askew, others with cracked gravestones, on towards the waiting grave.

He had moved with infallibility towards a crowd with a bottle in their possession. In the scant protection of convenient bushes they drank a bottle of joep. With watery eyes they joined the others at the gaping hole. He took one of the shovels passed among them. He heaped it heavily with sand and swung. The force of his swing catapulted him into the grave. Luckily the grave was almost filled and his flight was short. He raised himself on his knees, head level with a row of shoes, and stared at the outraged faces of the relatives. The jeering laughter of his drinking cronies mocked his predicament.

'The wife should've seen it. They had my number. There I was and under me the coffin, and if some mambarra had shovelled more sand in, I would've been buried with the corpse in the coffin. It would've been a case of two for the price of one — two corpses in one grave.'

The story of his escapade was greeted with silence by the old woman, whose fingers fluttered faster to pin the flowers on the wooden cross. The rest of the audience was more appreciative. The girls sat with twinkling eyes and found it difficult to control their squirming bodies.

'Many's the time the two of us had a puff of dagga together.' He paused for the old woman to understand whom he meant, and in order to make it quite clear he waved a hand in the direction of the other room. 'Think of all the occasions we've been together, the good times we've had, all the girls we've been with — what times! He was always a sweet bra, and now he's dead in his coffin!'

'Stop it!' the old woman screamed. 'Shut your disgusting mouth! Have you no respect for the dead! It's my grand-daughter, my beloved child, who's laying there cold in her coffin, while the likes of you go about spreading lies, lies, lies!'

The little girls, freed from the restraining glance of the woman, exploded in wild bursts of laughter.

Baby, That's the Way It Is

The two men lay wrapped in blankets neatly spaced apart as if they had marked out their territorial rights. Occasionally one or the other would raise his head as if to inspect whether anyone had encroached on his property. The door opened and a youth entered, the clanking and turning of a key shutting him in. The men raised their heads, and the light revealed that they were both well over fifty, if not in their early sixties. The youth swaggered over to the nearest man and nudged him in the ribs with his boot.

'Twak, wine swine!'

'No twak.'

'An' yer?'

The second old man shook his head.

'Yer wine swines never hef a ting. Long yer gotta bottle see-tru, yer okay. Christ! Two bags a shit ready to be dump.'

The youth strutted up and down the cell, stopped in front of the men and lit a cigarette.

'I gotta fadder like you, I piss on him. Yer stink up dis stinking place.' He pointed to the slops bucket in a corner. 'Doan know what stinks more, der shit bucket or yer two.'

He took a deep puff and the old man nearest looked longingly at the shortening cigarette.

'Gimme puff, son,' one of the old men whined. 'Man got no twak. I feella smoke.'

The youth finished the cigarette, dropped the stub in front of the old man and crushed it with the tip of his boot.

'Doan yer call me son, yer heappa shit!'

He kicked the old man in the ribs and laughed as he pulled his body away in pain.

'Only time yer here is when yer fill up wit' see-tru and it come out by yer balls! 'Morrow morning der law let yer go and 'morrow night yer back inside. Wine swines, all yer do is drink yer brain away!' The man he had kicked gave two wet coughs. 'Dat's right! Cough out yer lungs. Yer be dead long time orready.' He turned to the other old man. 'Wat say, olester? He go make out der night?'

The youth picked up two blankets from the pile and sat himself a little distance from the old men.

'How many times yer go to bud, yer two stink heaps?'

The old man he had kicked returned an indistinct mumble. The other man did not bother to reply.

The youth got up and towered above them.

'I speak to yer, olester. How many times yer go to bud?'

The man looked at him without flinching.

'More times yer be inside.'

'Dat's right. More times I be inside. An' everytime yer go inside, it 'cause yer drunk. Christ, der way yer wine swines go forra see-tru yer can piss inna glass an' get drunk on dat!' He resumed his seat. 'Yer know why I inside?' Neither of the men answered. 'Der law pick me up an' I hef my lem on me. Dey charge me wit' dangerous weapon. Doan worry me. Firs' ting 'morrow, my goose come pay der fine.'

Their lack of concern prickled him and he got up, swaggering.

'I know how to use a lem. Yer ever use a lem?' He crouched, grabbed at his back pocket and swayed from side to side making stabbing motions with his right hand. 'Dat's how yer do it.' He lunged forward. 'Inna guts. Dat's der way to give it to dem!'

The man who had refused to be cowed by his stare turned on his back and covered his head with his blanket.

The youth strode angrily over to him and ripped the blanket away.

'Doan yer believe me, yer old bastard? I gotta lem now, I show yer. Cut yer up quick. Only ting is dair be more see-tru running from yer den blood.'

'Yer can do it to me now but yer doan do it to me when I yer age,' the old man said calmly. 'I do ten years in Cinderella. I killa man an' I do it alone. Jus' der two of us wif lems. Wat yer wanna tell me 'bout lems?'

'Shit off, olester,' the youth said disbelievingly. 'Wair yer get dat head?'

'Lighties tink dey know everything.'

The youth grabbed the old man by the shirt-front. 'Who yer lighty, yer ole fucker?'

The cell door opened and a husky young man entered. He watched the scene. The youth turned to face the newcomer, who stooped to pick up a blanket, then approached them.

'Heit, Jonas,' the old man greeted.

'Watsa matter, Fietas?'

'Dis lighty wanna try his stungs wif me.'

Jonas confronted the youth and said in a pleasant

voice, 'Why for yer wanna do dat? Yer know Fietas?'

The youth shook his head. Jonas slapped him, sending the youth reeling. The youth ran around the cell trying to evade Jonas. The old man who had been the first victim of the youth's aggression sat up and cackled his approval. Jonas trapped the youth, slapped him again and threw him to the ground in front of Fietas. Then he took a seat between the two old men.

'Wair yer from, lighty?'

'Bokaap,' the youth snivelled.

'Wat yer in for?'

'Dangerous weapon.'

'Yer mean? Hear dat, Fietas? Dangerous burg. Wat dey catch yer wit', panga?'

'Lem.'

The youth rose and arranged his clothes.

'Sit down, moffie cart,' Jonas said, voice still pleasant. 'Who der hell tell yer to get up?'

The youth hurriedly seated himself.

'Yer a mobster?' Jonas continued his interrogation.

The youth shook his head violently in denial.

'Yer notta mobster but yer carry dangerous weapon.' Jonas turned to his companions. 'Maybe he a homeguard?'

They laughed at the cowering youth.

'We put yer on trial,' Jonas said. 'Fietas, wat's der charge?'

'Assault, muh Lord!'

'Any witness to der assault?'

'Yes, muh Lord,' Fietas's friend asserted.

'How do yer plea?'

The youth looked bewilderedly at the three men.

'As a member of der jury,' Jonas said to Fietas's friend, 'will yer tell der prisoner dat he must plead guilty or not guilty, or furder shut up an' get kick in der balls.'

'Yer hef to plea guilty or not guilty. It's der rules of der court. If yer gimme a smoke, I take yer case on.'

'Der pris'ner hef no right to hef twak,' Jonas commanded. 'Orderly, take away his twak.'

Fietas went through the pockets of the youth, placed a packet of cigarettes in front of Jonas and resumed his seat.

'Pris'ner, how do yer plea? Guilty or not guilty?'

'Not guilty.'

Fietas got up and smacked the youth.

'As orderly of der court, I mus' ask der pris'ner to call der judge "muh Lord" when he speaks to der judge.'

'Not guilty, muh Lord,' the youth said, eyeing Fietas warily.

'Hef der pris'ner gotta lawyer?' Jonas asked solicitously.

'I can talk for myself, muh Lord.'

'If dat's in order wit' der court, yer can precede.'

'Yes, muh Lord,' Fietas said in concordance, his friend nodding in assent as he balefully glared at the youth.

'Now let's hear der evidence. Fietas, yer swear to speak der trute and nothing but der trute, so help me God?'

'Yes, muh Lord.'

'Dat go for yer also, pris'ner,' Jonas reminded the youth.

'I was laying here mindin' nobody's business wen I was assaulted by der pris'ner to do me griebous bodily harm.'

'Was dair any witness to dis griebous bodily harm?'

'Yes, muh Lord. I see der pris'ner assault Fietas. Der pris'ner also kick me, muh Lord.'

'As I was party to seeing der pris'ner lay his hands on Fietas,' Jonas added, 'a man everybody know an' respect, dair no need forra pris'ner to plea. Der pris'ner must get up before sentence is pass.' The youth hurriedly got to his feet. 'Der court fine der pris'ner guilty of griebous bodily harm an' sentence him to be kick in der arse. Der court also claim his twak an' any udder personal property. Pris'ner, sit down.'

Jonas picked up the cigarettes as the prisoner sat down. Fietas moved in and slapped the youth twice while the other old man tugged at a jersey which came under the heading of 'other personal property'. The youth resisted, but reluctantly removed the jersey when Jonas smiled at him. Fietas's friend took off his torn jacket and pulled the jersey over his narrow shoulders. The youth looked at the jacket at his feet, moved around it and disconsolately sat himself down apart from them.

Jonas and the old man sat smoking; the new owner of the jersey lovingly rubbed its surface.

'Tings doan change,' Fietas said. 'It still der same der time I in Cinderella. Only dair you get real men, not snot-nose lighties like dat one,' pointing to the youth on the other side of the cell.

'Fietas was long time in der trade,' Jonas said to the youth. 'Fietas, in his days, issa hubba burg. You take him too lightly.' He lit a cigarette and tossed it to the youth. 'Dat's der trouble wit' people.'

The cell door opened and two men staggered in. They were well-dressed and looked as if they had come from a party. One had a piece of coloured streamer dangling from his breast pocket. He gave a nervous giggle while his friend looked apprehensively at the occupants in the cell.

'Come'n in, genemin,' Jonas said genially.

They weaved warily towards Jonas and the old men.

'Sit down.'

They sank down on their haunches.

'Wat's yer name?' Jonas asked, pointing to the one who wore the streamer as decoration.

'I'm Bruce.'

'An' yer friend?'

'He's Clive.'

'Clive an' Bruce, huh! Yer look nice an' high. Yer had a nice time?'

'We were at the engagement party of a friend of ours,' Clive responded. 'My car ran out of petrol so I locked it and we were looking for a garage. We had some whisky which we finished off, and then the police found Bruce piddling against the wall. They picked us up and here we are.'

Bruce gave out another nervous giggle.

'What's dis piddle business?' the man with the newly-acquired jersey asked, puzzled.

'He pissed,' Clive clarified.

'Den why yer doan say piss an' get finish wit' it!' the man replied querulously.

'Firs' time here forra two of yer?' Jonas asked.

'Yes,' Clive replied.

Under cover of the questioning, the youth had infiltrated and found himself a place in the midst of Jonas and the old men.

'To show we all friends here, we go hef a party,' said Jonas. 'Now, yer can get the party going by giving us a number, Bruce. Sing us a party song.'

Bruce looked appealingly at Clive for support. Clive focused his eyes on the floor. Reluctantly Bruce started singing in a quavery voice. The song ended and the old men clapped.

'Fietas,' Jonas commented, 'I tink we can get

Bruce to sing forra Ragtimes at Hartleyvale. Come'n, Clive. Show us what yer do in der dancing. Bruce, give us a number forra Clive to do der dancing.'

Bruce started singing with more timbre and Clive hesitantly danced, the old men clapping in time. The song ended, catching Clive off-balance. The youth sniggered at the two men's discomfort.

'Yer got twak?' Fietas asked.

Bruce and Clive hurriedly produced a packet each which Fietas passed to Jonas. Jonas shared the cigarettes in six equal parts. They lit up.

'Yer lucky, yer wit' friends,' Jonas said. 'Yer end up inna raman yard, yer in bad trouble. Inna morning, yer two an' Fietas an' olester walk outta here, free. I sit' cause dey catch me wit' a parcel gunston.'

'What's gunston?' Bruce asked innocently.

The youth looked at him in contempt. 'Dagga, yer kroets!' the youth said disgustedly.

'Won't there be any fine?' Clive asked.

'Der law shit dey catch yer wit' gunston,' Jonas replied.

Bruce started singing without being asked. Fietas's companion got up and motioned to Bruce to rise. The old man embraced him and they started dancing, Bruce still singing.

A warder's voice came from outside the cell: 'If you don't shut up, I'll come in there and shut up the whole damn lot of you!'

The warder's command silenced the singing and Bruce and his partner resumed their seats.

'Tell us about der party,' Jonas prompted.

Bruce looked at Clive, who shrugged his shoulders.

'The party was in Salt River, top part of Rochester Road,' Bruce said. 'Do you know Rochester Road?'

'Yer tink we farm boys?' the youth retorted. 'Dat's wair der whities stay.'

'We stayded there first before the Europeans moved in,' Clive interjected.

'It was one of the best parties I've been to,' Bruce continued. 'There was not a bit of trouble.' His eyes had a dreamy look. 'And the girls, they were fabulous.'

The youth shifted nearer.

'Clive, you remember those two wearing identical halterneck dresses? They certainly didn't need a bra.'

'I see some whitie goosies wear dress like dat,' the youth said, his hand reaching for his crotch. 'Did yer see dair tits?'

'Their tits weren't exactly hanging out,' Clive commented drily.

'Fuck yer!' the youth snapped as their laughter slapped him.

The door opened once more and a slender young man entered the cell.

The youth, to assert himself and regain his lost status, advanced towards the newcomer.

'Nice jacket yer hef, I tink I grip it.'

The newcomer slapped the outstretched hand aside and said, 'Cunt-face, yer thnk yer talking to a lightie?' Then he punched the youth viciously in the stomach dropping him to his knees. He placed his heel on the youth's shoulder and pushed him to the floor.

The youth's arrogance was replaced by fear as he looked appealingly at Jonas.

Jonas smiled appreciatively at the newcomer's action, and the two old men hooted their derision with cackling laughter at the youth's discomfit. The two party-goers were filled with apprehension at the sudden violence.

'How goes it, Sonnyboy?' Jonas asked.

'It's grand, Jonas. Two stupids near the corner try to show me dey men so I just had to put my lem into dem to slow dey lighties. But not to worry. I go to court tomorrow morning, I got witness to say dose two stupids try to rob me. So I pay a fine and back on the street I go. What's yer problem, Jonas?'

'Dey catch me carry a parcel of gunston. Gunston's heavy, so I doan see you for sometime. As you say. Not to worry. I know my way inside.'

'Fuck de law! What's cunt-face story?' Sonnyboy said, pointing to the sprawled youth.

'De law catch him with a lem,' Fietas said. 'An' he come in here act like a mobster to me.'

'So dat's his story.' Sonnyboy turned towards the sprawling youth and said; 'Hey, cunt-face, Come here.'

The youth hesitantly approached Sonnyboy.

'Go pick up six blankets and make a bed forra two of us.'

Jonas smiled as the youth spread blankets in a corner. The two old men cackled their glee. The two party-goers reflected their puzzlement.

'I tell yer to make a bed forra two of us, not two beds,' Sonnyboy admonished the youth, 'An' take off yer clothes. You go be my woman, cunt-face!'

The Homecoming of Mr Brown

'Tiena was here.'

He looked at his wife, then turned his face away and walked past her towards the bedroom. He took off his cap and coat and sank onto the bed. He stared at his worn shoes, sunk his head into the palms of his hands, and closed his eyes tightly. The many times his wife had said in the same tone of voice, 'Tiena was here.' Always it was Tiena who was sent, as if they knew he could not refuse her, the baby of the family. If only I could remain like this, never open my eyes, never have to comply with another request. Then he raised his head. His wife was framed in the doorway.

'What did she want?' His voice without a lilt, lifeless.

'The old man is in trouble, jail, and they want to get him out.'

'Jail?' He felt physically ill. His father in jail. He had never been there himself, but he knew all about it. He had been told about it so often by those who had been inside. Now his father was there.

'How much?' he asked.

'Five rand.'

'Jesus Christ!'

They might just as well have asked for fifty rands.

He did not have it.

'Haven't they got anything at all?'

She shook her head.

He stared at the wall with the paint rubbed off in places. Christ, of the bleeding heart, framed, looked at him with compassion-filled eyes. The royal family, posed in a semi-circle, all smiled sweetly.

From the other side of the wall his mother and father stared past him, starched and proper in their wedding clothes.

'Christ! What am I to do? Where am I to get the bloody money from?' The last an angry, anguished cry. 'Tell me? Tell me?' He held out his hands, palms upwards.

'I don't know,' his wife said softly. His hands dropped to his sides. 'Tiena said that the old man was on his way home, drunk, when he was picked up. They didn't know about it until this afternoon when another man who was inside came to the house. The message he brought from him was that his son should come and fetch him.'

He groaned. His father was inside and he was to get him out. He silently cursed the old man for the faith placed in him.

'Are you sure Tiena didn't bring any money with her?' He knew what the answer would be but could not help hoping that this time perhaps it would be different.

'She came without money.'

Frustration gave way to anger and was vivid on his face.

'Do you want something to eat?'

He did not reply and his wife left the room. He stared at the floor, cheeks pulled in and breathing noisily through his nose.

His father was older than his sixty-two years, the surface of his face creased and wrinkled, the skin hanging slack and eyes rheumy, the will long broken in the struggle to exist. He looked further back, to his childhood, and recalled the things that had destroyed his father — the things from which his father had tried to escape, only to discover he could never keep them at bay. Poverty and struggle, for a wage that would never clothe and feed the brood his parents had bred. Hunger and cold were unwanted members of the family.

Laughter was an infrequent visitor to their home. Love was there, but not much laughter. Laughter came hard when cold seeped through thin clothing and the thought of food filled the mouth with saliva and the lack of it brought a pain to the pit of the stomach. They had love, but not much to laugh over.

'Come 'n, eat.'

A place was made for him at the table. There was a plate with two fried maasbankers on it, potato chips, and a slice of bread fried in the same oil. A mug steamed with black coffee. He sat and poked listlessly at the food, his appetite dispersed by the news Tiena had brought. The food balled in his throat and he swallowed draughts of coffee to wash it down.

'Where's Tonie and Willie?'

'They've gone with Tiena. She went along to Sophia. She said she'll see if she can't get anything from them.'

'Little chance of that, with the number of children Sophia and that fool of a man of hers got. They don't get enough to keep themselves. Where would they get the money from? Not that I blame him, poor bastard! He tries hard.' His voice turned bitter. 'You'd think that Sophia would've more sense. She saw what happened to us. A house filled with children and nothing to feed them. But then they say a poor man's sport is to see who can bring the most children into the world.' He gave a short laugh devoid of mirth.

He looked at his wife. Her face was still unlined and the eyes direct. Most of his sisters had been aged prematurely by child-bearing. He had vowed that his two sons were family enough for his wife and himself.

He knew that he could not raise himself much higher than the station in life he had obtained. A steady job with the council, a pension at the end of his work term, and the slight possibility of retiring as assistant-foreman of his line-gang.

His dreams were invested in his two boys. Already he had brought them away from the slum streets where he had spent his childhood and come to manhood. His council cottage, one of thousands similarly structured on an enclosed plot of ground, gave him a feeling of permanency. He even had a garden. But his boys were his special pride. They would go much further. He would see to that. They would finish their schooling. Obtain the things of which he could only dream.

'Did Tiena have enough money to take them with her?'

'I gave her ten cents. I was going to use it to buy sweets and a ball for them, but they kept on asking to go along. You know how they are when they want a thing.'

He gave an indulgent smile, remembering how the two boys wheedled favours out of him.

'Look,' his wife said hesitantly, 'I still have the one rand thirty for the furniture, and then there's the twenty-five cents for the burial, and fifty cents for old Katz for the shoes he brought you and the boys. I can tell them to come next week if you want to use it.'

He did not reply immediately. The money she

offered was half of what was needed, and even if he took it they would be faced with the problem of replacing it the following week.

'I don't know,' he replied, his mind torn between the debt confronting him and the plight of his father in jail. Another night must not pass with the old man still inside. 'I'll take it.'

'Don't worry,' his wife said encouragingly, 'we can make out. It will be meatless stew and mealie meal for the next two weeks, but it won't kill us.'

He could not speak, his chest tight with gratitude at her calm acceptance of things. He said jokingly, to hide the feelings inside him: 'That's right. It won't kill us.'

They discussed, or rather he suggested, which of the neighbours would be able to lend them sufficient to make up the required three rands to complete the fine.

'I don't think we should ask any of them,' his wife said. 'I don't want them to know our business. They're a gossipy lot. By the time their washing's on the line the whole neighbourhood will know that the old man's jailed for being drunk.'

'Then who do we try? You know they haven't any money at home, and you can bet Tiena will come back with a sad story from Sophia. That's about all we can expect from her.'

'What about going to town and asking Tommy Williams. He's always on the look-out for another customer, not that I want this to become a regular thing.'

'But he wants fifteen cents on a rand.'

'There's nothing we can do about it. The old man must be brought home. There's no one else to turn to.'

'I guess you're right. I'll wait for Tiena, then I'll go

along with her. I still have two bus coupons.' Now
that the problem had been solved and his father's
release was almost a certainty, he felt much lighter.
He got up. 'I'll have a look at the dahlias. Did you get
Tonie to water them?'

'I had to water them myself.'

'Why?'

'They were fighting over it. Willie wouldn't let
Tonie do it unless he was allowed to do it first.'

He chuckled. 'I'll have to give Willie a talk. He
shouldn't try to boss his elder brother.'

'Much good it will do. I know your talks. And
when you hit them it seems that you're more hurt
than them.'

They laughed together and he left the kitchen.

He squatted in front of the row of dahlias, his
fingers tenderly stroking their thin stalks. His eyes
delighted in the feast of colour. On the other side of
the fence a man was connecting hose to tap. 'How are
yours coming on?' he called out. 'Not so good,' was
the reply. 'I waited too long before getting my bulbs
into the ground.' They traded information.

The gate opened with a squeak and he turned just
in time to grab hold of the two boys as they flung
themselves at him. Their force bore him to the
ground. He pretended to be angry and pushed them
from him.

'Willie, why didn't you let Tonie water the flowers?
It's his job.'

The young boy hung his head, bottom lip quivering.
'He said he wasn't going to let me do it too, daddy,'
he piped.

'Now, I'll tell you what to do. Tonight, Tonie
waters the flowers, and tomorrow night you do it. Is
that fair enough?'

They nodded in agreement and he dipped his fingers into the woolly hair covering their scalps. Beyond them stood Tiena and his sister, Sophia, a paper bag dangling at her side.

He took two cents from his pocket and gave each boy one. They ran inside to tell their mother. With Sophia and Tiena, he followed the boys into the house.

Sophia placed the bag on the table. 'There's a slab of stale fruit cake and three doughnuts. It's all right if you take it with your coffee.' She reached inside her coat pocket and produced three rand notes which she held out to him. 'Take it.'

Surprise made him stupid and he could only stare at the three notes curled around her fingers.

'How come you've got money, Sophia?' his wife asked.

'I'm working. I've got a half-day char and Lettie's working at a tea-room. She brought home the cake.'

'Karel been working this week?' he asked.

'Yes. They made him a regular at the docks. There's no need for him to slip ten cents a day into the palm of the Sarang to see that he gets a day's work.'

'Rhoda,' he started. His wife turned towards the dresser and raised the top of the teapot with the broken spout and shoved her fingers inside. She turned with two rand notes fluttering in her hand.

'Here,' she said, 'now we don't need anyone else. We can take care of it ourselves.'

He went into the bedroom to collect his cap and coat.

His wife shooshed the boys outside after handing each half a doughnut.

'Sit down,' his wife told her sister-in-law. Turning to Tiena, she added, 'You cut cake while I heat some coffee.'

Rhoda looked at her sister-in-law. Her bulk was covered by a shapeless dress, her neck cradled in pillows of fat, the three chins quivering as she spoke. Although it was not hot, her armpits were stained with half-moons of sweat.

'What's your madam like, Sophia?'

'She's not bad. She started with their usual nonsense, putting odd cents all over the place then checking to see if I'd taken any. I soon put a stop to that! "Madam," I told her, "if it's a thief you're looking for, you've got the wrong party! I'm not in the habit of stretching my fingers for stuff that don't belong to me." Now, there's no fuss.

'She even lets me have some of my money before the month is out, and you know how they can go on about that. Most of them will make you wait until the end of the month, and the mean ones make as if they'd forgotten and you have to ask for it. I'd rather work for a Jew, any time. Once they know they can trust you, they treat you right. The English are nice as pie, but to them you're always a child — a child big enough to see to their wants. For a Boer I'll never work. You must baas and nooi them the whole day long — and for what? They pay you the least and work you the most, and even then they're not satisfied!'

'I'm glad I don't have to work for any of them. Hard as it is for us, Willie don't want me to go out and work. He says I've got enough to do cleaning and feeding us.'

'You're lucky. With the lot I got, every penny counts. If I can get one of the boys in a job and nothing happens to us, then I'll be able to get shoes and something decent for them to wear at the end of the year.'

'The cake's ready, Sis Rhoda,' Tiena interrupted.

'Call Willie. Tell him he can have some coffee before

he goes.'

Tiena walked to the bedroom and stood in the doorway as Willie fidgeted with his cap in front of the mirror.

'Sis Rhoda says she poured some coffee for you.'

He turned around to face her. 'Tell her I'm coming.' Even the few, casual words were coated with the feeling of tenderness her presence engendered. The pinched face shadowed by the too luxuriant growth of hair covering her scalp; the bright eyes staring from that small area; her slight frame clothed in the thin cotton dress — another one he must shelter behind the wall of love he had erected to shield his wife and children.

'Here's your coffee,' Rhoda said. The remaining doughnut was placed in a chipped saucer next to the enamel mug. 'Sophia is going with Tiena,' she continued. 'I can take the children with, if you give me the two tickets. There's still ten cents over from the money I gave you. Ask Johnny, next door, for his bike. You know he stays home Saturday afternoons. We'll wait for you and the old man.'

'You think Johnny will let me have his bike? You know how he is with his stuff.'

'I'll go and ask him. You get done.'

He dunked his doughnut and hurried it towards his mouth before it could break in two. She was back before he had finished his coffee.

'It's all right. You can take the bike.'

He swallowed the rest of the coffee and rose from the table. 'I'll meet you at the house,' he said as he left them.

The bicycle leaned against the fence. He took hold of the handle and wheeled it away. 'Thanks, Johnny,' he called to the figure kneeling among the dahlias.

He pedalled away stiffly. His thoughts were with

his father. When the hell is he going to stop drinking?
It's bad enough that he doesn't care a damn what we
say or think but at least he should consider the effect
on the children. I don't want to see him, their grandfather, drunk as a sot, unable to control himself. I'm
doing my best for them. How would he like it if they
showed him no respect?

A picture of his father reeling up a street, coat
torn, pursued by jeering bands of children pelting him
with decayed vegetables snatched from garbage pails,
angered him. He pedalled furiously.

He parked his bicycle carefully at the entrance of
the non-white section of the charge office. The white
section occupied three-quarters of the space. The
bench in the non-white section was full, and draped
along the wall were men and women with faces
screwed into tight expressions showing a collective
sorrow. The white section was empty except for a
cat which lounged regally on a bench.

He stood at the counter and coughed deferentially.
The three policemen looked at him, then turned their
eyes back to the newspaper they were reading. He
remained standing. One of them raised his head and
stared at him intimidatingly. He backed away and
found himself a place amongst those leaning against
the wall.

A tall blond policeman with hair cropped short
moved towards the counter, leaned across it and
looked them over insolently. 'Why do you people give
us such a lot of trouble?' he asked no one in particular.
'What do you want?' He poked a finger at random.
'Who have you killed?' Willie started. 'Yes, you!'

He walked across the intervening space, fighting to
control the panic that set him atremble.

'Yes?'

'I've come to fetch my father.'

'Your father? Who's he? What's he done?'

'Tonie.' Then he stopped. 'Anthony Brown. He was drunk.' His voice lowered.

'Another dronklap! That's all you people do! If you don't stab each other with knives, you get drunk. We've got nothing else to do but look after you.'

All through the tirade he stood like a fear-filled pupil before a dreaded master.

'When was he picked up?'

'Yesterday afternoon.'

'Why don't you let him stay inside for the weekend? He'll only be back again. You know how you coloured folk are on a Saturday night, forever drunk.'

Willie did not reply. He clenched five rand in his pocket. The policeman scanned the register. 'Anthony Brown. 310 Rose Street. Is that him?' Willie nodded his head. 'Five rand fine.'

Willie edged the money across the counter. The money was gathered, a receipt made out and thrust at him.

The policeman strode towards a door leading to a passage. 'Anthony Brown! Fine paid!' he bawled, then turned, facing Willie. 'You. Outside!'

Those remaining looked hopefully at the policeman who returned their gaze with unconcealed contempt before resuming his seat.

A mammoth door, next to the charge office, was open. He could see a vast square within. A convict, wearing a red flannel jersey and knee-length khaki shorts, walked listlessly at the far end, a mop across his shoulder and a pail dangling at his side. He watched the convict disappear through a door and he shivered uncontrollably.

A small, iron door at the side of the square was

flung open and his father emerged. He looked at the figure coming towards him, clothing crumpled, and hatless, hair pointing to the heavens, and what looked like a smear of dried blood across a cheek. His mind veered away from what he had been told; of the beatings dealt out to those unable to defend themselves. Age did not count.

His father stopped in front of him. 'You came, Willie,' he said matter-of-factly.

Rage restrained by the policeman in the charge office burst out in sharp, bitter words. 'Yes! I came as I must every time come when you feel like getting into a mess. What the hell do you care. Whenever did you care? Get drunk like a sot and damn the rest of us! What about Willie and Tonie? Do you want them to grow up knowing that their grandfather is nothing but an old drunk! Is that the way you want them to remember you?'

His father did not answer and looked past him. Passers-by were startled by his outburst. 'Let's get away from here!' he snapped at his father. He walked towards the bicycle and without a backward glance to see whether the old man was following, he pushed it away.

He did not glance at his father who kept pace on the pavement as he pushed the bicycle through the streets emptied of traffic. He's right, the old man reasoned. I can't let the children see me like that. Not only little Willie and Tonie. Also the other children. He smoothed the front of his coat and pulled his fingers through his hair. He's a good son. Time and again he has come when I needed him. He made a few abortive attempts at speech which his son ignored. They continued the rest of the walk in silence.

The condition of their surroundings deteriorated as

they progressed; neatness gave way to decay. Streets were filled with screaming children whose intentions seemed suicidal as they flung themselves in front of approaching cars and recklessly hung from the backs of speeding lorries.

The house they entered was as decrepit as its neighbours. The smell of countless cabbage stews and fried fish suppers assaulted their nostrils as they walked down the passage. The odour was at its strongest in the kitchen. They could almost taste the stale fat. The old man made for his customary seat next to the stove. His mother, his wife, and Sophia were seated at the table. 'Coffee,' was his father's greeting to them.

He could not contain himself any longer. 'Is that all you have to say? Coffee! What about the worry you caused mother? What if we couldn't have raised the money to get you out?

'Because of you, we have to suffer. We know you've grown old working for us. But that doesn't mean we have to be satisfied with everything you do!' He made a final appeal. 'All we can spare we pass on to you. Is it too much to ask of you, to stop your damn drinking?'

His father sat with hands clasping the mug, cheeks sucked in as he sipped the hot coffee. The mug emptied, he held it out and requested: 'Coffee!'

Their mother knew it was her husband's way of letting her know that he had missed her. She smiled at him as she filled the mug with the grit-filled, black coffee.

Even Sophia's placidness was shocked by the old man's composure. 'It's true what Willie's saying. Papa is far too old for this nonsense. How can we ever face people if something happens to papa while papa's drunk?'

Tonie and Willie entered the kitchen. The old man

gathered them to him. The younger boy balanced on his knee and the other one stood between his legs.

'Close your eyes.' He rummaged in his pocket and withdrew two sticky toffees wrapped in paper. 'Here, take this.' He placed it in their hands.

They squealed their thanks, jaws working industriously.

Willie looked at his father and at his sons, and his anger was defeated.

Tribute to a Humble Man

His hands gripped the suitcases as he was swept along in the crowd. They passed the police station where he had been told he would discover the exact location of the street in Bonteheuwel Township where he was to lodge with a cousin of his father. He tried to free himself from the crush of bodies but gave up and allowed himself to be carried along.

More people joined them and the flow turned into a torrent. He looked at the faces around him and wondered at their grief.

The crowd stopped in front of a double-storeyed house with a balcony, the street filled from end to end. He had to crane his head to see what was happening at the front of the house.

His attention was caught by the appearance of people on the balcony. They were mainly women. Two white photographers moved to the front of the balcony and balanced against the iron balustrade, taking photographs of the women, who were all weeping.

The crowd hushed as a young boy, prayer cap on his head, positioned himself in front of the women. He cupped his hands around his mouth and performed

Athaan — the call to prayer.

The prayer was taken up by the crowd, the boy's purity of tone soaring above their mingled voices. Then the voice broke in its sorrow and plummeted. It was the signal for the women to increase the sound of their wailing.

Behind him a voice said that the boy was a pupil of Imam Haron. Another voice clamoured against the two photographers. They should desist from taking photographs of the sorrowing women.

A traffic constable inadvertently revved the engine of his motorcycle and was peremptorily rapped on his helmet. His white face flushed, the engine dying with an apologetic cough.

Scattered among the crowd were several males dressed in flowing, white linen robes, heads covered by prayer caps, a tasbeesh draped around each neck, fingers caressing the beads. It was one of them who had protested volubly against the presence of the photographers on the balcony.

He listened to the conversation around him. The name of Imam Haron was constantly repeated. Slowly the pattern formed.

Imam Haron was a Muslim religious leader who had died in prison.

Those crowded around the door fell back as the bier moved out of the doorway into the crowd. The wailing of the women rose above the subdued roar of the crowd. A photographer stalked the sobbing boy and more voices called angrily for his removal.

The crowd, the width of the street, followed the bier as it was carried on the shoulders of six men to an enclosed sports ground. The distance from the house to the sports ground was less than four blocks but progress was so slow that there were several exchanges of carriers before their burden was placed in the centre of the field.

A wide circle formed around the bier and the mourners who would deliver eulogies. The stand was swarming with people and all available space on the terraces filled. A prayer was said in Arabic and picked up by the crowd, who were mainly Muslim.

He discovered that those wearing hats, and the women present, were not Muslim. When he asked a grim-faced, elderly man why so many people were present, he was handed a newspaper. Biographical details and events leading to the death of Imam Haron filled the front page and overflowed to the other pages. He had been arrested on the birthday of Prophet Mohammed, the man who had introduced a new religion to the world — Islam. Arrested under the Terrorism Act, he had been imprisoned without being brought to trial. The newspaper stated that he had died of injuries caused by falling down a flight of stairs. There seemed to have been some difficulty as to when the Imam died, and there had been a delay in letting his family know about his death.

He was profoundly moved by what was happening around him. The most devout man that he could recollect in their village was not the priest but the father of his friend, Sarel. The father, like the son, was a shepherd who seldom came down into the village from the mountain pastures where he tended his flock. He conducted prayers for the shepherds, and not once would he allow any shepherd to bring wine or dagga into the camp. Imam Haron seemed to have shared some of the same qualities displayed by Sarel's father.

He looked at the people. It was the first time that he had left his home in the village to come to a place so large, with so many people. He had arrived on the early train from Johannesburg that had made a brief stop at the little siding of Ventersdal, where he had joined it. He had stood on the platform with his two suitcases, his father and mother, an assortment of aunts and uncles, and a few of his friends. His mother, face wet with tears, clung to him as the train topped the crest of the rails leading to the siding. In the short while that the train idled there as goods were loaded and unloaded, he went through a series of handclasps from the males and wet-cheeked hugs from the females. His father squeezed his hand hard, the only evidence of his emotion at their parting. He had not had a chance to say good-bye properly to Sarel. Then he had been on the train, searching for Sarel's face as the train picked up speed after a series of jolts.

'Did you know the Imam?' he asked his elderly companion.

'Yes, I knew Imam Haron,' the old man said. 'I knew him while he was still staying in Claremont. I'm not a Muslim, but then Imam had a lot of friends who were not of his religion.' The old man told him of how Imam Haron was always ready to help anyone in need of aid, no matter what their race or religion. He, for one, did not believe that the Imam had died from falling down a flight of stairs.

The old man pointed an accusing finger at the report.

'There, you can see for yourself. Imam was examined by a doctor the day before he died. He was declared fit. Now they want to tell us that Imam died after falling down a few steps!'

They had never concerned themselves with politics in the village. They had read the reports of injustices inflicted upon blacks by laws passed in a white parliament but, mainly because they were isolated from the mainstream and were decently treated by the farmers who employed them, these injustices had seemed vague. Occasionally, at school, a young teacher would exclaim angrily at a banning or imprisonment, and, invariably, the young protester would be removed from his post without any reason being given to the staff or pupils.

Another paragraph stated that up to that time fifty-three people had been banned. He was appalled to discover how many people had died in prison without being brought to trial. It struck him as strange that the cause of death in most cases was suicide.

Imam Haron was detained under the Terrorism Act but surely the authorities must have been mistaken. In spite of having grown up in a remote village and having attended a country school, he was not altogether unfamiliar with the politics of the land. If all these people felt the same way about Imam Haron as the elderly man next to him, then surely the Imam must have been a good man, a man Sarel's father would have welcomed to his mountain pasture, and in whose care he would have felt his sheep secure.

His feelings gave way to revolt against the measures used by the authorities to detain the Imam. The bier left the sports ground for the cemetery, the cortege worming its way to the main road. Faces crowded the pavement and all the shops were closed — another manifestation of the people's feeling towards the dead man.

A precedent was set by the number of women who had joined the funeral procession. It was not only Muslims who followed the bier. Those who walked were from all walks of life; labourers in greasy overalls jostled businessmen; an old man, bent with age, was helped along by his two grandsons; Christian students, briefcases bulging with theological text books, rubbed shoulders with befezzed Muslims; there were many African faces in the crowd. Their grief united them.

An elderly woman, leaning across her front gate, remarked that it was the biggest funeral procession she had ever witnessed, even bigger than that of Dr Abdurahman.

He wondered who Dr Abdurahman was and why such a vast crowd should have attended his funeral.

Three traffic constables astride their motor-cycles were at the head of the procession. Traffic came to a standstill as more than five thousand people followed the bier.

By the time it reached the main road leading to the cemetery, more than 30 000 people had formed an almost unending line. It was a funeral procession of a stature Cape Town had not witnessed for many, many years. The city would probably never see its like again.

As the bier moved slowly along, those on the pavement joined the procession.

The road was filled with more people than he had ever seen in his life. The smallest fraction of the crowd was greater than the sum of the people in his village, even counting those who came there at Easter time to augment the worshippers in their church nestled at the foot of the slope decorated with tombstones.

Women wept openly. A black nursing sister at a rest home for elderly white women fled the pavement sobbing. She was comforted by some of the inmates inside the grounds of the home. Three barefoot boys wearing oversized anoraks had accompanied the bier from the sports ground. The eldest one cautioned the other two to take care lest their khofijas be blown away by the wind.

'La-ilaaha Illal-lah, Mohama-dar-Rasoolul-lah,' they chanted over and over as they walked, the chant taken up by those standing on the pavements.

The five miles from the sports ground to the cemetery were covered in something over three hours. The cemetery could not contain the thousands of people and they spilled out on to the steep incline leading to the cemetery and the main road below.

More eulogies were delivered at the graveside. Overhead, a helicopter droned like a giant wasp. Someone remarked that the authorities were keeping their distance, and he realised that during the march he had at no point seen a uniformed policeman, except for the traffic constables.

Several men wept as the grave was filled. Slowly the crowd dispersed from the cemetery. He joined a group that was walking back to Athlone and listened to them as they spoke about Imam Haron. One said that the dead man would not have approved of the homage paid him; that he was a simple man, a man of the people though he was often in the company of those ranked higher.

He looked at their faces as he walked. His family had decided that he should attend the coloured university at Bellville and study to become a teacher. If he was going to protest against bannings and imprisonments without trial then his tenure as a teacher would not last long. And he was certain that whatever the nature of his studies, they would lead in the same direction as Imam Haron had taken.

Colour Blind

All the houses were identical in size and shape. Row
upon row, they filled the township with drab uniformity; by twos and threes, rows of squat adjoining
houses set in loose sand that made the growing of
flowers and plants a frustrating task.

In the kitchen of one of the houses sat a fifty-year-
old woman cradling a baby in her arms.

'Ooh, you lovely boy,' she said, 'Isn't he a darling?
He's his granny's favourite lollipop.' She hugged the
baby to her breast. 'No one's got such a lovely boy
like we've got. Isn't that right, Marcel? Whose grand-
son in Manenberg has blue eyes? You tell me, hey?
Oh, I could eat you.'

She sang softly,

> *My little fair-haired child*
> *With eyes so very blue*
> *your people came from*
> *over the wild seas*
> *and one day, you, too,*
> *will cross the stormy seas . . . .*

A knock at the door interrupted her singing. The

door swung open to reveal her neighbour.

'Morning, Stef.'

'Morning, Freda,' she replied, in a not altogether enthusiastic manner.

'You know, Stef. I don't know what sort of home these people come out. You lucky on this side. Last night they were fighting again. And the words they use. I tell you, Stef. That woman got no shame! And how they manage with all the children they got! Every night you see Mr Appolis come up the street with his bottle. I don't know how he can drink a bottle of wine every night the Lord give us, Stef.'

'Freda, I've told you once, and I've told you a hundred times! Stop calling me, Stef! My name is Stephanie! Stef is so common!'

Her annoyance showed in her face.

Not looking very concerned, Freda replied: 'Sorry, Stef — I mean Stephanie. It's just that Mr Appolis and Mrs Appolis work on my nerves. Their fighting and Mr Appolis with his drinking. It's not right! The white people in the City Council should come'n see where they put you. My late husband never touch a drop when he was married to me. Now I got to put up with neighbours who drink and fight every night. It's not right!'

'Yes, Freda. Every Jaap-Skraap is put next to decent people. Where we used to stay in Observatory, it was very nice. We lived among the Europeans. They called me Mrs Valentine. They showed respect for me. Not like here! The people who stay in this road, I wouldn't have them in my house in Observatory. Not that I have them here. I don't mix with the likes of them!'

'I'm sitting here,' Freda said, affronted.

'I don't mean you, Freda.'

'You right, Stephanie. Everyone off the streets is dumped next to us. And did you hear of Mrs Brown's daughter, at the end of the road?'

'Which family are the Browns?'

'They at the end of the road where you turn to go to the shop. The house with the two boards in the window.'

'I don't know Mrs Brown.' Stephanie creased her brow to locate the house. 'Is it the same woman who's always sitting in the doorway when I go past? I never greet her. Sitting in the doorway, mind you. Not even on a chair. Most probably she hasn't got a decent chair in the house. What happened to her daughter?'

'She's going to have a baby. She's already six months gone but you don't hear when the wedding's going to be.'

Stephanie shook her head reproachfully.

'Freda, you're right. These people have no shame!'

'And the boy who got her like that walk in and out of the house as if nothing had happened.'

'Want some coffee, Freda?'

'Yes, Stephanie.'

'Here, hold Marcel. I'll pour you a cup.'

Freda gave the child she held in her arms a disinterested look and inspected the tip of her shoe.

With a suppressed sigh of relief Freda exchanged the baby for the cup of coffee.

'What kind of coffee is this?' she asked, lips pulled back, showing her gums. 'It's not as good as instant coffee. Don't you buy instant coffee?'

'Of course, we buy instant coffee,' Stephanie replied huffily. 'It's just that we ran out of coffee and Miranda bought this last night.'

'One thing about my son. It never happen with us.

He buy enough groceries to last us a month. Sometime, there's stuff over. But then Willa's a good provider. If you run short, just knock at the back door.' She took a packet of cigarettes from her pocket, lit one and passed the packet to Stephanie. 'Did you see that coat Willa's wife is wearing? It's leather! Willa's not tight with money!'

Stephanie, to cover her agitation, held the baby in front of her, scrutinising its features.

'I think Marcel's going to take after his father. Not that Marcel is dark. All my children are light. My other daughter, Maureen, can pass. I always tell them they must make use of their colour and be careful the type of friends they have.' Looking archly at her companion, she added, 'Don't you think so, Freda?'

'My Willa got no white skin but he make more money than a lot of half-naartjies!' Freda retorted.

'My father came from England. We still have family there. I can remember letters and photographs my father showed us of our family. When my father died, the letters and photographs were lost, but I still have my father's birth certificate.'

Not to be outdone by Stephanie's forebears, Freda said haughtily: 'My people also come from oversea. My grandmother was from St. Helena. We may be black but we got no Bushman hair! We got straight hair! I can still hear my grandmother's voice. She speak English beautifully. Far better than your Observatory types. I grow up in Simonstown before we move to Newlands. I know how to behave myself with white people.'

'Were you sleeping in at the white people?' Stephanie asked, feigning innocence.

'I did not! I charred three times a week. There's nothing wrong with charring. All of us did. Girls from the farm sleep in. We owned our little cottage in Newlands. My madam was very good to me. She always ask about the children. Christmas Eve, all the young boys and girls sing carols at the big houses. My madam said she and her family always look forward to our children singing carols at Christmas Eve.'

'I've never worked for another woman,' Stephanie said smugly.

'You don't think I work for the whites you stay with in Observatory. I seen them. They not proper whites! They all poor white trash!'

'They didn't have the fancy houses like where you charred but they didn't treat me as a coloured char! They treated me like a white woman! I didn't have to call any of them madam! And when I visited them, I had tea in the front room just like the rest of their friends.'

'And look where you staying now. Manenberg! And all your neighbours are black and drunk! You know what the bible say? "Beware those who are proud. They will fall low!" '

Stephanie let her eyes travel the length of Freda's body.

'Did you come here to preach to me? I know what the Bible says!'

'I just want you to know that you not speaking to Mrs Appolis! I'm not like that! I come out of a decent home! Manners go a long way!'

'I'm sorry, Freda. It's just that I get mad with everything around here.'

'That's all right, Stef.' She pushed the packet of cigarettes over to Stephanie. 'Here. Take it! I still got half carton Willa bought me.'

Stephanie grudgingly took the cigarettes.

'Thanks, Freda. Why did they have to move us here

instead of placing us with people who are used to a decent way of living?'

'Then why don't you move?'

'How can we? Miranda and Claude got to work and there never seems to be enough money to put aside.'

'We going to move one of these days,' Freda said grandly.

'When?' Stephanie asked, not able to control the envy she felt.

'It won't be very long, now. Willa almost paid off the plot he bought in Fairways, then he go to the building society and we move, and I can say good riddance to Mrs Appolis and her drunken husband!'

'You're going to stay in Fairways?' Stephanie's voice sounded her doubt.

'That's right! We going to stay in Fairways. I know what you thinking. How can people like us who got no blue eyes and blond hair go stay in Fairways. My Willa with his black skin is getting more money than your Miranda and her husband can ever make. I'm sick of you and your white skin that is not even white! We going to stay in Fairways and all those half-whites will have to call me Mrs Oliphant because we got a home just like them!'

'I wish we could also move,' Stephanie said, getting up and placing the baby in a wicker basket resting on two chairs. 'If we had the money, we'd go to England. Miranda, Marcel, Claude and me.' Her voice filled with yearning. 'We'd go to our family and Marcel would grow up among his own people.' Then her anger and frustration spilled out. 'And I wouldn't have to look upon the likes of those in this street again!'

'There's also coloureds and blacks in England. Even Indians from India. What you do then?'

'You can be sure that we won't be staying among them when we're in England. My father said our family's staying in a small town in the country and when he came to South Africa,' — she paused and looked at Freda — 'it was the first time he'd seen so many dark people.'

'What about your Maureen, the one who can pass? Why don't you take her and her lot with you?'

'Her husband won't let her go with us.'

'But don't he want her to go to the land of her white grandfather?'

'They stay in Parow,' Stephanie said with complacency. 'Her children go to a white school.'

'She married to a Boer?' Freda asked incredulously.

'Yes.'

'So that's why they don't come and visit you while you been staying here for the past three years. When you staying in Observatory, it was all right for her and the children to visit their grandmother but now you stay in Manenberg they don't want to know you.'

'It's not Maureen's fault,' Stephanie said hurriedly. 'I told her not to bring her children here. I don't want them to see us like this. You know what happens when it's Friday or Saturday. Last week they killed a man in the street behind us. You understand, don't you, Freda?'

Freda answered reluctantly: 'I know what you mean, Stef. But still, it's not right! Don't you ever see them, now?'

'I sometimes see Maureen. She writes to me and I go to town and wait for her in the gardens, in the Avenue. She brings her little baby along. She's a few months older than Marcel. Her name is Michelle. She's a lovely child, although she hasn't blue eyes like Marcel. At least, Maureen's children are saved from having to grow up here.'

Freda got up and gave the kitchen a critical look-over.

'Why don't you get Miranda's husband to buy you a new fridge? This is a old model. Willa bought us one where you don't have to worry about the freezer. It work automatic and it got space for frozen food.'

'There's nothing wrong with the fridge!' Stephanie said indignantly.

'Willa's wife said that Willa must also get us a new kitchen set to match. Not that our kitchen set is old. Willa buy the set two years ago and he pay cash money for it, mind you. But Willa said when we move into our new house, his wife will have a new set. He'll also buy a kitchen dining set. Just like the ones in the big houses in Newlands. And we'll move in with a new car. He's going to trade in our car when we go. What do you think of that, Stef?'

'That's nice,' Stephanie said sourly.

'You know what, Stef? I tell Willa to sell you our kitchen set when we move out. I know you appreciate it. It will remind you of me every time you take out a plate from the dresser. It cost Willa over a hundred rand when he bought it new. When you buy from the Jew, it's going to cost a lot more when you pay it off. That's another reason why Willa never buy things that way. He says why make the Jew rich?'

Stephanie, unable to contain her exasperation, burst out: 'Freda, must you always brag about the money Willa's got and the things he buys?'

'You not jealous are you, Stephanie?'

'How could I be jealous of a . . . .'

'Go on, say it! How can you be jealous of a colour-ed? You think you and your daughter, with her husband, and your white skins are better than us!'

Freda got up and angrily pushed the chair aside so that it fell to the floor.

'Your daughter and her husband, white skin and all, can't even get you out of here! And your daughter, Maureen, is ashamed to come and visit you because you stay in Manenberg!'

Stephanie also got up and moved towards the sleeping baby in the wicker basket.

'I see that I've made a mistake, Freda. You're no better than Mrs Appolis and the rest!'

'Don't you tell me that I'm like Mrs Appolis! I come from a decent home!' Freda shrieked.

'You're not acting like someone from a decent home. You're acting common, just like the dirt in this street! I'm afraid that you have to leave my home! You're upsetting Marcel.'

'Common!' Freda shrilled. 'You tell me I'm common when you grow up with your white trash and pretend that you as good as they. You know what you are, Stef? You even lower than your poor white trash. That's what you are. Not-even-poor-white trash!'

She stomped towards the door and slammed it behind her.

'You black bitch!' Stephanie screamed venomously.

Bitter-sweet Memories

The summer sun trailing fingers of heat touched the balcony and roused them from sleep. They looked at each other and exchanged sleepy grins. Stretching lazily they tossed their single blanket aside to reveal bare chests and lower limbs clothed in white satin long trousers, garish with vivid red and yellow stripes, mementoes of coon carnival days.

From within came sounds of the tenement coming to life.

'How about breakfast?' Sonnyboy asked.

'Here,' Walla replied, nudging with his foot a small demijohn in which swirled three inches of white wine, 'have some see-through.'

Sonnyboy spilled some wine in a cup and with a circular motion of the wrist rinsed it. He tossed the dregs over the balcony, then filled the cup. He passed the cup to his companion.

One of the men ready for work stepped on to the balcony and looked at them drinking.

'What about work?' he asked them.

'Naw,' Walla answered, 'I win a screw on the dice at the club. The old lady got her money for the week, so I don't got to make like a horse. Have a dop before you move to the dump.'

'Thanks,' he said, reaching for the cup. 'Sonnyboy, you also making it ladies' day?'

'As Walla say. He make the money on the game. Besides, I got three days clear and Walla's old lady not going to panic if I'm short.'

'It's going to be hot in the hold today,' Walla said conversationally.

'Ja,' their companion agreed, 'and we gotta sonofabitch offa Sarang. The docks is hell onna day like this.'

'The docks is hell any day,' Sonnyboy said laconically.

'What can you do if you got woman and kids?'

'Stop making kids,' Walla said drily.

'You mean I gotta sleep with my tool in my hand?'

Raucous laughter rumbled from their throats.

'Walla, gimme a rand. I see you right on Friday. I wanna buy two zolls from the merchant.'

Walla flipped a rand piece at him. 'Keep it. When I go broke, I bum from you.'

He left them reluctantly and a few minutes later appeared in the street below.

The street filled with people, work-bound: girls with scarves covering their hastily-combed hair and eyes still puffy with sleep, men carrying small pails which held their food. Their curved hands resembled the hooks hanging from the broad leather belts encircling their waists; they used these hooks to shift cargo in the ship's hold.

The wine at an end, Sonnyboy took out a zoll which he had placed inside his boot. He used his fingernail to slit open a cigarette and mixed the tobacco with the dagga. He rolled two sticks and handed one to Walla.

White wisps of smoke curled skywards and the

dagga crackled as the flame touched it.

'Slaves!' Sonnyboy jeered goodnaturedly at the workers passing in the street.

Walla's youngest brother peered through the doorway.

'Where my twenty cents?' he asked hopefully.

'The old lady got it.'

He shook his head. 'She don't give it to me.' Not budging from his position he stared steadfastly at Walla.

'Here,' Walla said, handing him twenty cents, 'you wanna cigarette?'

He nodded his head eagerly, pocketed the cigarette and the twenty cents, and hurried from the balcony before they could detain him further.

'They going to fresh air camp,' Walla explained.

Sonnyboy's mind flickered back to the last occasion that he had been to summer camp, or fresh air camp as they termed it. It was five years ago now, but all the times he had spent there had jumbled into a sprawling picture of confusion, so that he was never sure which incident had happened when. All that he was certain of was that it had been the best part of his childhood.

He recalled that the children of the tenement were the first to stir when it was time to go to fresh air camp, raising their heads cautiously to make out whether their parents were awake. Those who had fathers or older brothers working in the docks watched with ill-concealed impatience the slow preparations for work, and when their fathers and brothers had left the room they jumped out of bed and dressed with hurried movements.

They badgered their mothers to gather their things together, anxious not to be left behind. Brothers and sisters younger than themselves were unmercifully pulled from beneath the sheltering warmth of blankets and made to stand on legs slack with sleep while garments were wrenched off and slipped on to their bodies. Tears greeted the threat that they would not be taken along.

Soon the whole tenement was awake and those already dressed went from room to room whispering and nudging and getting in the way of flurried mothers driven to distraction by the demands of their own brood. The intruders were chased outside with sharp clackings of tongues but this did not deter them from moving on to the next room, from which they would be evicted seconds later.

Breakfast was another restraining halter and at its completion they bolted down the stairs and squatted outside on the pavement as if fearful that the tenement would turn into a trap.

'Look atta mob going,' Walla said.

A dozen children chattered noisily in front of the tenement. Small suitcases with blankets tied to them were piled in a heap. Two women emerged from the tenement and marshalled the children around them. Four more children came rushing to join them, a mother's strident voice in pursuit. Then they set off. Goodbyes were shouted by the rest of the mothers ranged around doorways.

Sonnyboy and Walla looked at each other and grinned. Then they leaned over the balcony and hollered at the departing children.

'Hell, wish I was going,' Sonnyboy said wistfully, puffing angrily at his stick, smoke coming from his nostrils like war clouds.

He could see them as they walked to the station. The white people they passed stared at them

curiously, eyes focused on their often-washed clothing and their bare feet. Tied to lapels and buttons
of dresses were short lengths of string, cardboard
discs bobbing at the ends, their passports to summer
camp.

They were oblivious of the stares directed at them,
happy in the thought of the ten days release from
over-crowded houses and confining rooms; rooms hot
at night, with bed-bugs crawling from underneath the
skirting boards and attacking flesh exposed to gain
relief from the stifling heat; walls smeared with the
blood of crushed bugs giving off a sweet-sickly odour;
rooms where privacy was an unheard-of thing, and
where the creaking of the bedsprings of their parents'
iron double-bed signalled awareness of life come early.
Around their necks fluttered the means of their
escape. If only for a short spell.

'I wonder ifa lotta kids still go?' Sonnyboy speculated.

'Ja. Bunny say all the kids sell papers to get tickets!'

'The station must be packed with 'em.'

Sonnyboy's mind tracked back to the platform
from which they had made their departure. About a
hundred children stood around, split into groups.
They joined them, forming another group. Their
number increased as yet more groups arrived. They
stood taking stock of one another. Even if their garb
did not betray them they would still have been re-
cognisable as from the back streets: big eyes bright in
thin, pinched faces. The few who were round-faced
and well-fed looked out of place among them.

Standing apart, as if to disassociate themselves
from the children, stood a half-dozen men and
women; school teachers with sheaves of paper in their
hands.

At the edge of it all, a handful of mothers smoothed hair and straightened jackets while the objects of their ministration writhed under their hands.

Through other entrances came more groups making for the platform, until every inch of space was covered with a whispering, giggling, elbow-jabbing mass of children.

The arrival of the train signalled a stampede. Doors were wrenched open and a scramble for seats ensued. Those more wise in the ways of travel hung back, knowing that when the third class carriages with their wooden seats were filled they could sit back in comfort on the padded sofas of the first class.

Those unfortunates who were seated facing the platform had to listen to last-minute instructions from the mothers at the windows, which they heard out with scarcely-concealed boredom. As the train pulled out they hastily withdrew from the windows to be spared the waved farewells; a last token of maternal anxiety.

Like warriors bound for conquest their singing spread from coach to coach. Their songs were the songs sung by coon troupes parading the streets of Cape Town at the New Year.

As the glistening twin steel tracks lengthened behind them their joy increased, finding expression in the ribald words introduced into the songs sung.

A teacher burst into the carriage to silence their ribaldry. A momentary hush marked her progress down the aisle, then the rows she had passed took up a chant referring to a section of her anatomy. Defeated by this new attack, she retreated from the carriage in a stiff-legged walk to control the offending part of her anatomy at which their verbal darts were aimed.

Steenberg, their destination: they tumbled out

excitedly, running up and down the platform before being unscrambled into lines and shepherded through the subway where two lorries waited.

The smaller children, together with all the suitcases, were placed aboard, and when the lorries pulled out their treble goodbyes quivered in the air.

'More dagga left?' Walla asked as he took a last drag at his stick.

'I still gotta finger in my hat.' Sonnyboy removed a small lump of brown paper from inside the leather sweat-band of his hat. 'Here,' he said, offering Walla the short end of his stick, 'I'll roll us another one.'

'I wonder they still got scouts at the camp?'

'Must be,' Sonnyboy replied. 'They like the law, always fucking up things for us.'

'Aw. They not so bad.'

The scouts that met them at the station hustled them into a procession. The procession had a very unmilitary look to it as it marched along the road stretching from the station. Two scouts were at the head. Flanking it was the rest of the patrol, with two more acting as a rearguard — all stiff with importance in their khaki uniforms and peaked hats. Marching songs whistled by the scouts and taken up by the marchers kept the column moving briskly.

Clear of the town, pavements were replaced by sandy patches. Sorties were made from the ranks to snatch at wild berries or juicy figs bursting at the sides. The two-mile walk was completed without effort.

A spontaneous roar erupted from them as they entered the camp. Smaller brothers and sisters were rescued from piles of suitcases.

Those of the boys who had been at the camp before left the younger ones to struggle with the baggage while they raced for the shed in which they were to sleep.

Fights flared and victors took possession of the choicer spots, the losers moving on to tackle lesser opposition. Blankets were spread and the shed assumed a lived-in appearance, the ground already littered with discarded sweet wrappers and odd socks. On the other side of the kitchen, dividing the shed into two sections, the girls had taken their positions with less friction and no fights, content to watch each other silently as they changed their clothes, each torn petticoat carefully noted for use in furthering or breaking friendships as the days went by.

The clang of iron-on-iron announced the call to eat. Mugs in hand they queued. Plates were heaped high with food and the mugs brim-filled with tea. The soft clatter of spoon against plate was the only sound heard, and those with big appetites were not denied a second helping. Bright eyes sparkled above raised spoons and stomachs expanded comfortably. Veterans of twelve and thirteen flaunted their knowledge of the camp while they ate. Those there for the first time listened attentively.

Time was spent making friends, while former friends split and new groups were formed, all vowing eternal friendship that would last only until they broke camp.

Night, after supper, brought on community singing and was the forerunner of other nights that would remain indelible in their memories, revived in later life if they should meet.

Sonnyboy lit a fresh stick and blew twin columns of smoke at Walla.

'Not even those damn scouts could block our sport.' This time Walla agreed. 'The things we did . . . .'

Sonnyboy's voice softened and a far-away look filled
his eyes.

The evening had faded into night. The lights of the
camp were doused. From underneath blankets rose
figures and marauding parties formed. Huge bull-frogs
captured during the day were released in the bed-
clothes of slumbering girls — then a stealthy retreat to
their own quarters to lie awake in anticipation of the
piercing screams that would come from the other side
of the shed, and the soothing tones of the scouts and
camp leaders quietening the terrified girls.

Raids were made in their own quarters as well, but
these were marked by the physical cruelty stronger
boys displayed to the weaker. Blankets were wrenched
off sleepers and their bodies lashed with belts. The
anguished cries of the victims brought the scouts
running, with torch beams cutting a swath through the
darkness. To escape from the stabbing torches hiding
places were found next to sleepers undisturbed by the
clamour.

Elaborate plans were made for the discomfort of
the few who suffered from the pangs of home-sickness.
They were salved with sympathy and told to stockpile
sandwiches for an escape from the camp in the middle
of the night. Led to the main road they would be
deserted and their defection reported to the camp
leader. Their wails heralded their return under escort,
the jeers of their betrayers their only farewells when
they were taken home the following morning.

Those were not all the delights the camp held:
getting up in the morning when the sun was still
without heat, and performing callisthenics with bony
chests proudly arched; long hikes to the beach,
chewing dried apricots; being elected camp orderly
and strutting around with a switch, in charge of a litter

squad; camp romances at the wash tap where extra status was gained by having your washing done by a girl not from your district. The wonder of it all — the hundred-and-one things that could not be done back home, where the street was the only playground.

Then, too soon, came the last day at camp. The sadness that crept into the last day's play, which not even the farewell concert could sweeten. It was time to leave. For those who had reached the age limit, it was a time of regret. For them it would not be a renewal of acquaintances next time. The camp was truly over, its halcyon days were done.

It was a subdued band that set out for the station. The cheery voices of the scouts held no comfort for them. Their eyes bleakly reflected their envy of the scouts who would remain until the camp closed to all visitors. They were going back to their tenements and the strangulation of the spirit. The time they had spent at the fresh air camp would assume a new wonder with each retelling until it was the legend of a happy part of childhood unblemished by the dark shadows that fell over growing up in the back streets of the city.

'Shit! Walla, tell me, must things change?'

'I don't know,' Walla replied, blowing a thick puff of dagga to hide the desolation on Sonnyboy's face. 'Things just change, that's all!'

Crucifixion

Around him, on the slopes of the hill, sheep grazed. A long-eared dog guarded them, red tongue hanging out and sides heaving. He stretched out a hand for the pig's bladder filled with water and a tremor ran down the length of his body. His fingers stiffened and he slid from the flat stone on which he rested. Eyes dilated, he lay staring at the sky.

Clouds took the shape of a man shrouded in a robe, head bare, with a long beard trailing to his waist. A voice boomed louder than thunder: 'JAN! You are the one!' Thrice it was repeated, then the clouds spilled apart and resumed a white nothingness.

A wet warmness brought him to consciousness. The dog towered above him, whining distractedly, its tongue caressing his cheeks. He dug his fingers in its coat and pulled himself to a sitting position. In front of him the sheep grazed calmly. Only the dog had sensed that something unaccountable had taken place. He fondled its ears.

'Dankie, Held,' he said, his controlled voice and soothing fingers assuring the dog that everything was as it should be.

An adventurous sheep attracted Held's attention as

it hopped stiff-legged away. The dog snapped at its heels in a mock display of anger, sending it scampering back to the safety of the flock.

He was filled with the wonder of it. To him all things were simple. It was either black or white. If there were any shades in between they escaped his simplicity.

A voice had spoken to him. It was no mortal voice but whether it had been the voice of God, he could not tell. The message was not clear but he did not doubt it. He was the chosen one. Chosen for what? He did not possess the answer. It was enough that it was said that he was the chosen one.

All through the afternoon his mind dwelt upon it and when the shadows showed how late it was, he got up reluctantly and with the aid of the dog moved the sheep to the sheltered section of the hill where the camp was.

Darkness came as suddenly as it does in the country. One instant it was still light, then all objects lost their familiar shapes and only his trained eye could make out their positions.

A dassie was impaled on a length of wire and broiled over the open fire. The dog lay drooling at his feet, anticipating the pleasure of crunched dassie bones. The dassie satisfied their hunger and he drank a mug of hot coffee, black, to end the meal. The dog jumped up to investigate the security of the flock now enclosed in a rough doring-bos kraal.

After one last look at the heavens, he wrapped himself in his blankets and was soon fast asleep.

They were on the move early the next day to fresh pastures. Each day the sheep grazed on a different section of the hill. Several times, during the passing of the day, he looked at the sky and was disappointed when no voice boomed.

A cloud of dust on the trail below told of one of the farmer's periodic visits. Five minutes later, he dismounted from the back of the prancing horse. He tossed the reins to Jan and moved into the shade. Jan advanced hat in hand after tying the horse's bridle to a bush.

'Môre, Baas Dirk.'

The farmer acknowledged the greeting with a grunt and a nod of the head. They walked towards the sheep, Jan a few paces behind. The farmer picked up a lamb and weighed it, placed it on the ground, cornered a ewe, sank his hand into its wool and smiled.

'Any losses from jackals?'

'No, baas. One lamb broke its leg and I had to kill it.'

'Or did you kill it because you like fresh mutton?'

'A good shepherd does not harm his flock.'

The sincerity of the words appeased the farmer. Without further speech, he turned on his heel and walked towards the tethered horse. He anticipated the prancing to follow as he placed a foot in the stirrups. He came down heavily on the horse's back when it reared, and tugged sharply at the reins so that the bit pressed into the soft velvet lining its mouth. The horse submitted and the farmer, pleased, inched it forward until the horse was almost on top of the shepherd. From his height he spoke.

'Ampies will be at your camp Saturday night. Two months from now, you bring all the sheep down to the farm for shearing, and God help you if there's a loss of lambs.' He wheeled his horse and sent it spurting with a slash of the riding crop. The shepherd was left coughing the dust thrown into his face by the hooves of the horse.

The voice spoke to him twice before the arrival of

Ampies and each time his body stiffened and he fell
to the ground with eyes wildly staring, unseeing.
Nothing was added to the message. He was still the
chosen one. That was all. The dog had become
accustomed to his sudden collapses and no longer
stood whining at his side.

Saturday night brought Ampies with the supplies.
'Baas Dirk sent you food. He also said for you to
remember his warning about the lambs at shearing
time.' Ampies also brought news of the punishment
which had fallen on Boeta Haas.

' "Haas has befouled the fair day of the Lord,"
Baas Dirk said "and he must be punished! All of you
come outside and bear witness to what befalls those
who heed not the words of the Lord and myself, his
servant." And although we were preparing for prayers,
we had to follow him like children and share in the
shame of Boeta Haas.

'Boeta Haas was under the tree near the dam, unaware of our presence. Baas Dirk plucked the shirt
from the back of Boeta Haas and slashed him all over
the body with a heavy switch, all the time shouting
that Boeta Haas, in his drunken state, was like the
swine possessed by demons that had fled into the sea.

'Baas Dirk was so filled with the Spirit that I feared
that he might command us to pitch Boeta Haas into
the dam.

'Some of the women wept when blood flowed
from the back of Boeta Haas, and Baas Dirk told
them to stop their weeping and instead concern
themselves with guarding their children from falling
into slothful ways like their elders.

'We carried Boeta Haas home after Baas Dirk left.
Every Sunday morning early, we have to attend
service in the big house.'

Ampies raised the bottle after his long recital and greedily drained it of its contents.

'Ampies, will you listen to what I have to say?' Jan asked in a low voice. At first hesitant, then more assured, he spoke of the voice from the heavens.

Ampies looked at him with a doubtful countenance. 'Are you sure the lonely days and nights have not affected your mind?'

'No, Ampies. There is no . . . .' He fell backwards, body stiffening.

Ampies threw the blanket from him and jumped across the intervening space. He dropped to his knees beside Jan and raised his head. Except for the dilated eyes, Jan had the appearance of one in deep slumber or dead.

'Magtig, Jan! What's the matter?' Ampies whimpered. He looked around him as if to draw aid from the surrounding darkness. Near him lay the dog with eyes half-closed, mouth opened in a contented grin. Ampies's fear soared when Jan failed to respond to his ministration and, to relieve his strained nerves, he cursed the dog who answered him with a wag of its tail.

A moan from the rigid body assured him that Jan was still with the living.

Jan's open eyes and calm manner angered him, and to hide his anger he accused Jan of secretly drinking.

'Did you hear it? It was wonderfully clear. Like organ music we hear in the church in the dorp.'

Ampies shook his head. 'I didn't hear a thing.'

Ampies was short and slight of build, and his features showed his mixed blood: nose flat, the nostrils round caverns, slit eyes; his complexion a muddy yellow-brown and his head covered with tight, crinkly curls. His age could have been anything between twenty-five and fifty.

He dropped to his knees and slid the heavy rucksack off his shoulders. Loosening the straps, he burrowed beneath the heavy parcel of foodstuff and withdrew a bottle of brackish wine.

'This is for me. It's all the food I want.'

While Jan busied himself transferring the supplies to the shed where he slept in bad weather, Ampies made himself comfortable in front of the fire. He raised the bottle to his mouth and the gurk-gurk of the flowing liquor told of his deep swallow. He rubbed his lips with the palm of his hand, gave a contented sigh and wriggled his buttocks deeper into the soft soil.

Jan took the blankets from the bed in the corner and walking towards the doorway of the shed asked, 'Are you going to sleep inside?'

'No. I'll sleep outside with you. On the farm, like a prisoner, I sleep in my cottage every night, rain or shine. I've almost forgotten how it feels to have the earth beneath me and the stars above.'

Jan tossed one of the blankets at Ampies who wrapped himself in it, leaving only his hands and the upper portion of his body free.

'You lucky that it's not every day you under the heavy fist of Baas Dirk. Every day the fist lands heavier on the neck of us volk. It's work from the moment the sun wakes until it slips from sight behind the kranse, and, even then, if it's still light, Baas Dirk finds more work, so that at night your body is so tired that there is no pleasure in joining the others for a last smoke, and you turn away from the enjoyment of your woman's body.'

He gave a deep sigh and peered at Jan for signs of sympathy. 'It is heavy, this life of ours!' Jan responded, and Ampies repeated: 'Yes, it is heavy, this life of ours!'

Another deep swallow, and Ampies continued:

'Saturday nights are no longer nights of enjoyment for us. Baas Dirk has forbidden us to have our pleasure late into the night. No longer, far into the night, do we hear the twang of guitar strings, and the young girls no longer entice the men of their choice with the swaying of their hips as they dance to the music. And, once, when Boeta Haas was found drunk on the Sabbath day, Baas Dirk came to the cottage of Tant Minna, where a bid-uur was held, and stood at the door.'

'The voice said that our necks will be pressed deeper into the dirt and the fist of our oppressor will grow heavier, but we need not despair. Soon I will know the honour that is to be mine, and then our suffering will be at an end. Tomorrow, you must tell the others of what I speak.' Jan rolled himself into his blanket and was soon asleep.

To Ampies sleep did not come so easily and far into the night he pondered over what had taken place.

He rose before the dawn but Jan was already busy at the fire and handed him a mug of coffee. The hot drink banished the chill of the morning air and Ampies swallowed it gratefully.

'I got to go so that I'll be in time for morning service, or else Baas Dirk's heavy hand will find my neck.'

Jan watched Ampies trudge down the hill.

With the aid of Held, he shepherded his flock to its pasture.

At the farm the service had just begun.

Dirk van Zyl stood at the end of the room, one hand resting on the table and the other clasping a heavy bible. Facing him was his family; his wife, his two sons, their wives, and children. At the back of the room, and lining the passage, were the farm workers. Ampies took his stand among them.

The sermon was a long one, and white and black writhed under it, as the self-appointed preacher and guardian of morals taxed them on their duty to a God whom he presented as stern and just, and certain to punish their transgressions with brimstone, fire and damnation. The sermon ended with a warning to the labourers to yield their will to him, Baas Dirk, their master by divine right.

Ampies, at the bid-uur later, reported the incident at the camp in the hills and, with the exception of Tant Minna and two women, all were sceptical of his report. Their recollections of Jan were of a quiet boy who grew up apart from the other children and whose parents were forever complaining that he seemed to live in a dream world. He preferred the solitude of the hills to the babble of humans, and when he obtained manhood, while others of his age courted and mated, he cut himself off further by taking the job as shepherd. Since then he had rarely been seen on the farm. He had yet to lie with a woman, to their knowledge. This fact, in their eyes, marked him as singular among males. Ampies insisted that his story was true and Tant Minna argued that all they had said clinched the issue. With whom but the pure in heart would a voice from the heavens converse?

Their minds still could not associate the silent Jan of their memories with the figure, painted by Ampies in his story, who would bring their suffering to an end. They decided that the three men should accompany Ampies on a visit to the camp in the hills.

Nightfall, the farm preparing for sleep, found four figures slipping from the workers' quarters and silently making their way past the outbuildings. They hushed a dog which barked when a light shone from a window in the big house, and quickened their pace once away from the farm. They had to be back well before sunrise when the others went to the fields. There was no time for resting. Nine miles were covered in one stretch.

With sweat-stained bodies and tired limbs they approached the camp. Ampies called apprehensively to Jan when a snarling Held confronted them. A whistle from Jan brought the dog slinking back to the still-smouldering fire. They came forward. Dried wood was thrown on the fire and it was soon ablaze. They squatted around it.

'They wouldn't believe me when I told them of what you've said.'

Jan looked at them. 'It is true. Every word of it. I would not lie.'

They recalled Tant Minna's words. Only to the pure in heart would a voice from the heavens make itself heard. Jan was known never to have uttered an untruth.

'When will there be an end to our sufferings?' 'What's going to happen?' 'What's this great honour you're going to receive?'

Jan shook his head. 'It has not yet been made known to me. When it is time, I shall know.'

They no longer doubted when they left the camp, although still uncertain as to what the voice could have meant. They said that they would visit Jan again. They hoped that he would reveal to them how the end of their sufferings would come about.

Word spread. They stood in groups while out in the fields, heads together, and when they broke apart they tackled their tasks with renewed vigour.

The barking of the farm dogs grew more frequent at night and the number of visitors to the camp in the

hills increased. After each visit their excitement
spread as the day of their release, according to Jan,
crept nearer.

The farmer observed their restlessness and took to
watching them, disturbed by the way they gathered
and stood whispering, and the unaccountable light of
joy in their faces.

Ampies grew in importance in the eyes of the rest.
He assumed the position of a disciple. Through him
all the news was relayed. He could hardly restrain
himself as he neared the farm one morning. He was to
tell them that at last they would know when their
suffering would end. When Jan had told him of the
plans the voice had, he had wanted to rush down to
the farm and shout the glad tidings for all to hear.

He was dejected when Jan made him promise not
to say more than that they should come to the camp
the following evening to hear the new tidings.

A figure detached itself from the shadows and
touched him on the shoulder as he passed the outbuildings. He turned and almost fell to his knees from
shock.

Dirk van Zyl, sjambok trailing from his right hand,
stood before him.

'Well, Ampies, and where do you come from?' The
voice held a quiet menace which could be felt.

'Nowhere, baas. I couldn't sleep any longer and
went for a walk.'

'And last night? And the night before, and the
many nights before that when you and the others left
the farm, only to return before the sun rose? Now,
tell me where you were, Ampies.'

'Nowhere, baas. I couldn't sleep.'

'Get in there.'

The sjambok pointed to the barn.

The farmer closed the door and drove Ampies into a corner with the sjambok. After four strokes the farmer stopped.

'Will you tell me now, Ampies?'

Ampies shook his head and was knocked down by a blow in the face. Blood streamed from his nostrils and the sjambok bounced off his body. The farmer paused for breath and Ampies whispered that soon all his suffering would be a thing of the past. The farmer stooped and grabbed hold of his coat collar, shaking him like an empty sack.

'What was that?'

'Ja, Baas Dirk,' he said defiantly, 'soon all our sufferings will be at an end, and the heavy yoke smashed from our necks, and Jan will lead us away from your bondage!' His eyes lit up as he spoke. 'The voice from the heavens told him that he is the one to lead us away from the land of our suffering, and that whoever raises his hand against Jan will be destroyed.'

The farmer was speechless at such a sacrilegious declaration. When he regained his voice he screamed hoarsely, 'Get out of here!'

Ampies told the crowd of anxious workers to prepare themselves. At nightfall he would lead them with their families and possessions to the camp in the hills from where the trek to freedom would start. There was nothing to fear from Baas Dirk.

Dirk van Zyl watched them from the window of his bedroom as they made their way to the fields. The blood rushed to his head, preventing clear thought. He ranted at his sons.

'There is a pestilence on our lands! The volk has the audacity to believe that the voice of God has made itself heard to Jan, the shepherd!' He paused for an instant to wipe away the froth forming at the sides of his mouth. 'To Jan the shepherd, the hotnot, and not to me, His dutiful servant! Do they think that God, if He should consent to speak to us, would use a hotnot as His mouthpiece? I forgave them when they drank and when they whored. But this, this I cannot forgive! On your knees, my sons.'

Hands aloft, he faced his kneeling sons. 'O Lord, hear the prayer of Thy vassal. Grant me the power to strike the fear of Thy wrath into the hearts of those misguided fools. Let me be Thy instrument, destroying those who lend their ears to blasphemous tales. Let my hand be the one that strikes down this hotnot . . . .'

His body, overcome with the fervour of his exhortation, shook with sobs. His sons left him to his weeping and joined the cowering women and children in the kitchen.

The workers were a silent lot as they waited for the day's ending. Dirk van Zyl, in the big house, kept to his room and spent his time praying and weeping. He was calmed when darkness fell, and stood watching the line of laden workers pass through the farm gate on their way to the camp in the hills. Ampies, slightly drunk, was in the lead, a bottle swinging from his hand.

Not a word was spoken during supper. The meal completed, Dirk van Zyl made a sign to his sons and they strode from the kitchen. They saddled their horses and rode out at a canter, sjamboks dangling from their saddle-horns. They slowed down once they were clear of the farm. Dirk van Zyl felt no urge to rush now that the vengeance of the Lord was at hand.

The camp site was filled to overflowing. They sat in a semi-circle, all eyes on Jan. The light from the fire played on his features; his voice, when he spoke, was gentle and carried to all of them.

'No more shall we suffer. The days of suffering are done with. It has been made known to me, this honour that is mine. I am to lead you on a trek to freedom. Away from the heavy hand of Baas Dirk.

'No longer shall we be used as oxen that they own, fit only for work. For no man shall own another and make of him a . . . .'

His words were interrupted by the clatter of hoof-beats. His hearers scrambled to their feet and scattered as the three riders rode into their midst.

A string of unintelligible words poured from the mouth of Dirk van Zyl as he slashed with his sjambok at the heads of those around him. He drove his horse at Jan and sent him spinning to the ground. The horse reared, and repeatedly he brought its front hooves drumming down on the sprawled shepherd who lay helpless under the flailing hooves.

His sons rounded up those of the workers who had not managed to flee. Dirk van Zyl jumped off his horse and ordered his sons to pick Jan up and bind him to a doring-bos. They tied his hands with leather thongs so that he hung between two trees, the thorns pressing into his arms, his feet free of the ground. A gleam in his eyes, the farmer addressed his workers.

'Now, you will see what the Lord has commanded me to do!' He marched towards Jan. 'Hotnot! You dare presume that God would converse with you?' Each word was punctuated by a blow from the sjambok and wrung a scream of pain from the crushed body of the shepherd.

Ampies moved forward but was stopped by a sjambok slash across his face. The others who watched Jan's scourging gave themselves up to keening.

Dirk van Zyl continued the beating until he was tired and no sound came from the mouth of Jan.

Then he and his sons drove Ampies and the others back to the farm like so many sheep.

Jan raised his head once and moaned for water. His moan went unanswered. Then his head sank on to his breast and his body swayed as the wind sported with it. The dog returned to the camp and sat on its haunches beneath him. Pointing its mouth to the sky, it howled its sorrow to the night.

The Awakening

'Herman! Help laai die lorrie, ons gaan Kaap toe.'

'Ja, baas,' the man replied, placing the sack of potatoes next to the door of the big, white farm house. He joined the others stacking a three-ton lorry with carrots. They listened to him as he supervised the work. He was young, lacking two months to complete twenty-four winters, and of medium height. Manual work had broadened his body, his face was wide and pleasant, and his hair hung in wiry curls like the wool of a sheep ready for the shearer.

The farmer watched them from the front as they threw a huge tarpaulin over the carrots and fastened the edges to the side of the lorry. A voice arrogant with ownership instructed them as to their duties in his absence.

Herman stood next to a woman a head shorter and one or two years younger, his arm around her waist. In front of them two boys played. The elder showed, in the stance of his body, that in later years he would be as Herman was now. Herman smiled as the younger boy snatched at the clay ox in his brother's hand.

'Klim in, Herman.'

He fondled the heads of his sons and smiled at

their mother, then climbed in on the other side of the cab. The lorry pulled away with a grating of gears and the workers drifted back to their toil. The two boys stood with their toes dug into the soil and waved at the lorry hidden behind a curtain of dust.

The dirt road was replaced by one of smooth asphalt bordered by fields of crops interspaced with fruit trees. Clumps of sheep grazed beneath the trees and at the end of a field a stallion mounted a mare while the rest of the herd looked on without interest.

The farmlands fell from view, replaced by groves of trees whenever they approached a small town. Beyond each town, the road would seem to stop dead at the top of a steep incline, only to appear again as they crested it, plunge downwards, and vanish again at the top of the next rise.

Traffic became heavier as they approached the outskirts of Cape Town's northern suburbs.

The farmer swung on to the freeway system. On either side of the road now, a hundred metres or so from its edge, shanty towns were clustered. Herman looked with revulsion at the poverty around him, comparing it with the cleanliness of the farm cottages.

Half an hour later, they pulled to a halt in front of one of the gigantic warehouses at Epping market.

Panel vans, lorries large and small, horse carts, and even push carts were crowded together in front of the warehouses. A small army of boys, all ragged, surrounded the lorry and made it known that they were willing to help unload. Herman got out of the cab just in time to prevent a youth from snatching a bunch of carrots.

Each time he came to Cape Town with the farmer, Herman was amazed at the hugeness of the crowd and its noise. Not even New Year brought so many people to their tiny village.

A small boy, dirty shirt draped over the top of his trousers, had a grimy hand on a large carrot. Herman looked at him sternly. The boy smiled disarmingly. Herman could not resist the smile, remembering his sons on the farm. The charmer in the dirty shirt walked away, vigorously munching at the large carrot.

Herman supervised the off-loading and when the last load of carrots was trundled into the warehouse, the farmer, after signing a consignment note, motioned to him and he climbed into the lorry.

A ten-minute drive brought them to the Grand Parade where they parted. The farmer took a bulky pile of letters and papers from the dashboard and shoved it down the inside pocket of his coat. A line of cars obstructed his progress from Herman's view.

On his right, behind the marble statue of a dignitary long dead, a group of people surrounded a lone speaker, bible aloft, who exhorted them to find salvation in the blood of the lamb. A guitar struck up after the speaker had finished and a hymn was sung by his circle. None of the people standing around joined in the singing.

Herman's interest was caught by three students wearing black capes who approached the worshippers and those gathered around them. Two of the students were girls, one white, the other black; the third was a white youth. They carried sheaves of pamphlets which they distributed.

He searched the face of the black girl to detect the unease he would have felt if he were to walk in such close proximity to a white, and in apparent friendship. He could not understand the naturalness of the situation.

The black girl approached the lorry, smiled, and

handed him a pamphlet. He gave a tentative smile in return. He watched the three students as they disappeared behind a row of cars.

'WAGES' printed in big, bold letters headed the pamphlet's message.

The arrival of the farmer prevented further perusal and he hurriedly placed the pamphlet in a pocket hidden from the farmer's sight.

The journey back, for Herman, was a thought-provoking one, his mind filled with what he had seen and heard. It was late afternoon when they reached the farm. He was sent to check the last chores of the workers. At sundown he hurried to the cottage shared with his father, his wife and his two sons.

Like the other cottages, his was built of clay coated with unslaked lime and roofed with thatch. Two windows flanked the front door. The kitchen was at the back, and also served as a dining room.

Maria was busy at the fireplace. His father joined them a few minutes later from the fields. The old man greeted them and disappeared into the room he shared with his grandsons. He did not come out until Maria announced that supper was ready.

The two children sat at the table, faces scrubbed and hands washed. Food in front of them, they sat with heads bowed as the old man said grace. Outside, shadows were deepening.

The meal ended, Herman and his father went to sit by the fire while Maria cleared the table and prepared the boys for bed. Dressed in coarse flannel night-shirts they kissed the two men goodnight.

Maria joined them at the fireplace. Herman brought out the pamphlet and placed it in front of her.

'Tell me what it says, Maria.'

He watched her as she read and was filled with

pride.

Her parents had had great hopes for her. She was their only child, and one of the few village children who had attended high school in the town ten miles from the village. The death of her father, when she was in standard eight, killed her dream of completing her schooling and becoming a teacher. Her mother, always sickly, soon joined her husband in the section of the cemetery set aside for them. Maria, after the death of her parents, was like one lost to her surroundings, and Herman, who had loved her since boyhood, hovered about her anxiously. One Sunday, after church, he approached her and with much hesitation asked her to marry him. He could scarcely believe his good fortune when she accepted. She joined him and his father after the wedding celebrated in the church hall. The farmer's gift was a lamb which they reared. When the farmer placed her in charge of the farm school, he felt that the world had given him its all. Maria his wife — and now, a school teacher.

She re-read the pamphlet before speaking in a low tone, as if afraid that her words might be carried outside and overheard.

'Herman. Father. This tells of the little money we are paid for the work we do. It also tells of the suffering of those who work the land.'

The two men showed their puzzlement.

'How are we suffering?' Herman asked.

'There are many ways in which we suffer, but because you've become accustomed to it, you can't see it.'

She pointed a finger at the pamphlet.

'Here, it says that things mustn't be the way they are. We should share in the good of the land and not, as now, be showered with the bad. It says that we, the workers of the land, must be paid decent wages and must live in better houses. It also says that the tot of wine the men get must be stopped. We must all come together and join in the struggle to make the land sunny for all of us.'

The old man shook his head.

'What's wrong, father?' Maria asked.

'I don't like it! From the beginning it was always like this. The white men rule and get everything, but if we listen to their words and obey, they will look after us, like Baas du Toit is doing. The people who say those things don't know us.

'Baas du Toit and me grow up together. I work under his father like my father work under his father's father. And now, as it should be, you are working under Baas du Toit, as you work under his son when he come from the big school in the city. Who give us this house to live? Who see that there is enough to eat and our mugs never empty of wine? And what of the ox that is slaughtered and the meat shared among us? No, my son. Don't listen to the words of those who know nothing of the way we live.'

Herman and Maria remained silent while the old man spoke. When he stopped, Maria looked at her husband.

'What do you say, Herman?'

'I don't know,' he haltingly replied. 'I must think. Tell me more.'

The old man got up when Maria resumed speaking and left the kitchen murmuring under his breath.

Later, in the darkness of their room, Herman turned on his side and gently nudged Maria in the ribs.

'The girl who give me the paper was brown like us, and there she was with this white woman and man, speaking to them like Baas du Toit's daughter, jong nooi Wilhelmina, speak to her friends. It was so strange to see.'

The following morning found Herman in thoughtful mood as he worked, not joining in the laughter of the others. They had to repeat their words when they addressed him. One of his friends slipped an arm across his shoulder. Grinning slyly, he said, 'Is Maria with child?' Herman left them to their laughter and walked away.

At nightfall, after supper, Maria took out the pamphlet and told him more of what it said, and its meaning.

His father left them in the middle of Maria's explanations. During the nights that followed, the old man retired as soon as supper came to an end.

In the fields, as he worked, Herman let his mind dwell on conditions on the farm. They were fed and sheltered by the farmer but the cottages were of the same materials as built the stables and the kraals. They worked each day from sunrise until it was almost dark. They worked every day except Saturday afternoons and Sundays. For all their work they received little money and had no say in their lives.

He remembered how, once, one of the labourers had had an argument with the farmer. He had been thrown off the farm with his family. When he reported his treatment to the police, he was told that he was lucky they had not arrested him for leaving the service of his baas. A few months ago, when he had said that he would like his son to go to the school in the village, the farmer had told him that his son would go with the rest of the farm children to the farm school managed by his wife, Maria, where the children could be on hand when needed to help in the fields.

Maria had rebelled when he told her, but he feared to go against the farmer's command. He silenced her roughly when she said that they should leave the farm. To leave the farm and go against the word of Baas du Toit was too overwhelming an undertaking for him to tackle.

Her nightly explanations and teachings gave him new insight into their life on the farm and brought the outside world and its happenings closer.

When he returned one night he found the normally calm Maria aflutter with excitement. Not waiting to give them supper, she spread a newspaper on the table. It was four days old.

'Police Arrest Student for Distributing Pamphlets'. Underneath the headline was a picture. Herman looked at Maria.

'The police in Cape Town have arrested forty-three students. They say the students have been handing out pamphlets urging workers to go on strike for higher wages.'

He looked at the picture. One of the girls looked like the one who had given him the pamphlet but he was not certain.

The old man broke in. 'That is what happen to those who fight against the rule of the white man.' He turned to Herman. 'Beware, my son. It's not right to think that one day we'll sit at the same table with Baas du Toit.'

Supper was a hasty meal. Maria snatched each plate from the table as soon as they were done with it and dipped it into the basin of hot water.

An hour before midnight they were still awake. Maria did most of the talking while Herman listened, only speaking when a point was doubtful.

'We must go to the city,' Maria said softly. 'Here,

there is no future for our sons. You've seen that Baas
du Toit won't let your son go to school in the village.
He wants your children to grow up like the children
of the others: work animals with just sufficient mind
to be able to do their work.' She added fiercely, 'I
will not have it! They must get their chance. If they
go to a high school in Cape Town they will not end
up as slaves on a farm, fit for nothing but toil.'

The enormity of what Maria proposed frightened
Herman. What his father had said was true: on the
farm they were guarded from the outside world by
Baas du Toit. As long as they listened to him they had
nothing to fear from the police.

'What can I do?'

'You can easily get work in Cape Town. You can
drive a lorry. There must be work for a lorry driver. I
will not stay on the farm any longer.'

Her words strengthened him.

'It's for you and my sons that I will do it. They
must not grow up under the heel of the white man. I
will tell Baas du Toit.'

He wondered whether the young girl was among
those arrested.

Herman told his father of their decision in the
morning. The old man did not reply and hurried to
the fields without a backward glance.

Maria dressed the two boys in the clothes they wore
for going to church in the village. When told of their
destination they sat wide-eyed with the wonder of it.

Herman stood in the dust in front of the stoep, his
hat held in his hand. The farmer sat on the stoep in a
leather-thonged chair, a cup of coffee raised to his
mouth.

The farmer looked at him without speaking, taking
in his town attire and that of Maria and the children.

In the background was the sound of workers busy in the fields.

'Meneer du Toit.' The farmer stiffened at the omission of the customary 'baas' and looked hard at Herman. 'We are leaving the farm — Maria, me and the children. We are going to Cape Town.'

'What about your father?'

'He is staying.'

'You would leave the place of your birth, where the body of your father's father is buried and your children first saw the light of day? You would leave it all and go to Cape Town? Why?'

Herman did not reply. In spite of his resolution, he was still fearful of telling the farmer his reasons for wanting to leave the place where he was born. He had never thought that he would leave of his own free will.

'Leaving the farm is not as easy as you imagine. All I have to do is to ring for the police and they would lock you up.'

'I know.'

'And yet you would go?'

'Yes. They would not keep me locked up forever. And after it is done with, I could still go and you would not be able to stop me.'

They looked at each other. The farmer, eyes filled with anger, tried to impose his will upon Herman, to send him scampering to the fields to join the other workers. Herman returned his gaze without flinching. Maria had come closer to him and the children were silent.

'It is for the children that we are leaving,' Maria said boldly.

The farmer's eyes leaned on her then moved to the two boys who fidgeted under the weight of his gaze.

When he spoke, his voice did not reflect his rancour.

'Then go to the town! Go to the town where your children will grow up to become skollies, your wife a whore and you a drunkard! Go to the town where you will all die in filth!'

They walked down the dusty road, Herman carrying the two suitcases, his wife by his side and the two boys scampering ahead.

Three-way Split

They stood leaning against the wall of the public convenience on the Square, like trees felled in their prime and left to rot until they finally fall apart, brittle with age. Their vigil, in all kinds of weather, had left its mark on their faces.

A few of them still had the appearance of men, and when they raised their heads their eyes were bold, if a little dimmed. The others had the downtrodden air of beaten dogs. When spoken to they shuffled from foot to foot; they twisted and crumpled already shapeless caps in horny hands permanently moulded in the shape of hooks, even when they hung useless at their sides.

Their dress had a sort of uniformity. Black jackets shone with grease and age, trousers did not match. The collars of the jackets turned up to hide grimy shirts whose cuffs protruded from their wrists like over-sized price tags.

Their feet were covered by articles that were shoes in name only. Some were patched with thick pieces of cardboard which also served as inner soles. All that held the fragmented leather together was the string securing it. The uppers were torn, and through the cracks parts of their feet could be seen.

A car pulled into an empty space between a small sports model and a van. A ripple of interest stirred their ranks. Two of them shuffled forward.

They moved nearer as the white man got out of his car. Their voices were a soft, apologetic whine. 'Master, we clean your car for you?' The white man looked at their raggedness, noting every detail, then turned towards the car, a huge, shiny mound of metal. He nodded his head more out of pity than need, and turned away to avoid their words of gratitude.

A bucket was produced from its hiding place inside the iron palings encircling the solitary tree standing guard in front of the door on the men's side of the convenience, and from their pockets came an assortment of rags. They argued as to who was to fetch water from the tap on the other side of the Square.

The other vagrants stood watching as they argued, then lost interest and moved to the side of the convenience now favoured by the sun. They arranged themselves along the wall. The more enterprising claimed the choicer seats on top of wooden boxes placed against the wall.

There followed a general search in pockets for 'stompies'. Those who did not have any looked with longing eyes as the butts were puffed. When the smoker had difficulty in holding the butt it was reluctantly thrown away.

Now two of them were rubbing industriously at the surface of the already shiny car, and as they worked they talked in whispers of what they were going to do with the money, speculating on the amount. One was in favour of a certain cheap wine while the other selected a different brand, equally cheap. They debated the merits of their choice with the fervour of connoisseurs.

A final rub, and then they took their places in the sun with the others, placing themselves so that they were in a position to take part in the conversation and at the same time have a clear view of the Square.

The sun dropped behind Signal Hill, and like a tide advancing the shade crept up on them until it covered their entire section. They pulled their coat collars tighter against the chill in the air.

They thinned out one by one, shuffling off in different directions, saying no farewells, making no appointments, each knowing that the other would turn up before the bar opened at ten o'clock the next morning.

Only the two who had polished the car and one other were left. They eyed him, then cast meaningful glances at each other, reckoning in their minds the possibility of a three-way split.

No rules were made and no one spoke about it, but if there was ever anything to be shared, it was shared by all present. If one was to be excluded, it was done very thoroughly, leaving him alone in the wilderness.

They watched the white man as he walked across the Square, and by the time he reached the car they were waiting cap in hand.

The white man had difficulty with his tongue and slurred the words as he spoke. 'Here, buy yourself something to tide you over.' He slipped a silver coin into each of the outstretched hands and laughed as one of them dropped his coin.

The door of the car was closed with an action that was grotesque in its imitation of a uniformed commissionaire stationed at the entrance of a luxury hotel, and as the car pulled away they touched the peaks of their caps in salute.

They had enough to pay for the two bottles of cheap wine they craved, or one bottle of a better type which they knew their companion, standing a few yards away, would prefer. Advancing, they asked him his choice.

He was non-committal and shrugged his shoulders while they, like little children eager to please some one stronger, rattled off the names of all the wines they knew. They paused for an instant after each name and looked at him, but he said not a word. His lips were a thin line, lending more strength to his face. He was one of those who still had the appearance of a man: the grey stubble and the slightly hollowed cheeks only accentuated this quality. With the money in their hands they hurried away.

Their return was a series of short, eager steps. They carried the parcel between them. A sound of disgust fell from his lips when they removed the brown paper wrappings. There were two bottles. Their greed had been too much — they had not been able to resist buying two bottles of cheap wine instead of the bottle he would have approved of. They looked furtively at him but there was no further complaint.

Both bottles slipped from their grasp in their eagerness to get at the wine. The bottles were poised in mid-air for an agonising instant, then they fell to the ground. They shattered and the wine swirled at their feet.

They looked at the fragments of glass in disbelief. Then they hit out at each other with ineffective blows, screaming curses, their cheeks streaked with impotent tears.

He walked away, coat collar pulled tighter.

Azikwelwa

He did not have to walk. He looked over his shoulder at the hundreds coming along behind him, all walking, and in front of him hundreds more, walking. He was one of the few coloureds who walked along with the mass of Africans. They were old and young, big and small, foot-firm and limping, mothers and sons, fathers and daughters, grandparents and school children; some dressed in neat clothes with horn-rimmed glasses and attaché cases, and many in torn overalls and shoes with soles paper-thin, feeling each stone they trod on. They were all walking the long walk to Johannesburg.

Nights before the boycott was due, the location's fast-beating heart increased its pace. Wherever a man raised his voice, a group formed around him, and as the hours passed, there were many such groups until the location was one huge meeting place. There were the wild ones whose eyes only saw violence, and their cry was, 'Burn the buses!' Then there were those who whispered: 'Accept the terms.' But there were also the many who shouted defiantly, 'Azikwelwa! We will not ride!'

When they started their walk the sky was still dark

under the pulsating stars. He watched them from the inside of his room, and after a time went back to the warmth of his blankets. He had a bus to himself on the ride to the station. There were angry voices when he boarded the bus, but those who shouted the loudest were restrained by others with rosettes pinned to their breasts. Then, when the bus passed the long, firm line of walkers, he heard their cry again. His return from work found them homeward bound, a song travelling their length. A stone hit the side of the bus and he peered through the rear window. Four men were shaking a youth by the shoulders and they all disappeared from view as the bus turned a bend in the road.

As if by a prearranged plan, the location's streets swarmed with people who embraced each other and sang at the tops of their voices. In the backyards of the shebeen queens, skokiaan flowed freely for those who had the money to pay for it. And even those who came with empty pockets were given something for their thirst. As they faced one another they cried, 'Azikwelwa, my brother!'

Four days he watched them walk the long walk, and four nights he saw them dance and drink their aches away, and the spirit of their pride filled him. Their word was as good as that of the white man. They said they would walk the many miles before paying the extra penny the bus company demanded. There were many whites who scoffed at their determination, and this was their answer — the line of empty buses. He joined them on the fifth morning, when the first wave of walkers passed his door. From side streets poured rushes of walkers, and the mass of people flowed through the gates of the location.

On his left walked an old man who used a stick to

help him along and in front of him waddled a fat woman with a bundle of washing balanced on her head. He looked around him. There were many such women, and some of them had babies strapped to their backs, the heads of the babies jogging with the motion of their mothers' hips.

It was still early, the first mile not done, and they were in a holiday mood. Bicycles carried two passengers. The location's ancient cars, which always threatened to fall apart, were loaded to capacity and wheezed their way forward. One man, his boots tied around his neck, joked with his friend and said that it made for easier walking. All joined in the laughter. They were walking the long walk, and they were proud.

The miles passed and the road was long: there was less laughter, but still they walked. The old, the sick, the weak, dropped behind. The front of the column was wide but behind it tapered off to a thin line of stragglers.

Then suddenly there were the police and the cars standing in rows, the people inside pulled out and forced to the side of the road. The owners protested that the cars were not used as taxis, but they were still charged with overloading. There were harsh demands for passes, and the fear as they waited for the vans to take them away. Then the next block of police, waiting with outstretched hands and ready batons for those who had not the slips of paper which gave them the right to move. There were many who slipped down side streets to escape, for the police wanted them to ride and not walk, so that there would be no strength of will, and so that they should be without a voice.

'Pass! Waar is dit?' he was asked. The owner of the voice did not bother to look at him. Only when he did not reply, did he turn his eyes.

'I don't carry a pass.'

'Then what are you doing here?'

'I'm walking!'

'Are you a kaffir or are you a communist?'

'I am walking!'

He walked past the policeman who had already grasped another victim by the shirtfront, demanding his pass.

A large car pulled to a halt in front of him, behind the wheel a young white woman. She opened the doors on each side and called out, 'Come on. Women and old people.' No one moved. Then a woman with a child on her back and a suitcase in one hand shyly approached the car and got into the back. Others followed. The old man shook his head saying that he was not too old to finish the long walk. More cars stopped. Their drivers were white and they took those who wanted to ride.

One of them asked the young policeman by whose orders he had stopped a car and demanded the removal of the passengers. The policeman stood undecided and the car pulled away. The policeman rushed towards the nearest man and screamed, 'Julle kaffirs dink julle is slim!'

Messages were passed from those arrested, to assure an employer that an employee would come back to his job, to tell children not to worry and to help each other.

And those who walked were still many, and their hearts were heavy, but they walked. Then the long walk was at an end, for below them was the city. The people of the city looked at them with disbelief and their shoulders straightened and their heads lifted and they smiled. They had walked the long walk, one more day.

It was late when he entered the chemist shop where he worked as a messenger.

'Jonathan, why are you late?'

'I walked.'

'All the way?'

The white man looked at him with surprise.

'All the way!'

'But why? You're not one of them.'

He could not tell the white man of the feeling inside him, that when he was with them he knew it was good.

He joined them on the Square at mid-day. They sat with mugs of coffee and still-hot fat cakes bought from the portable coffee stalls of the vendors. Some sat around draught boards, using bottle caps as counters, but most were clustered around those with newspapers. There were pictures on the front page showing the many walkers. The reports stated that the boycott would soon be over and that the leaders of the boycott had come to an agreement. There were angry murmurs among them, and some said aloud that they did not believe it. One man said what they all had on their minds. 'Why is it that we were not approached? Are we not the people who walk? Does the bus company think that because it has spoken to a few men, we, like sheep, will now meekly ride instead of walk?'

The last question was directed at one who wore the colours of the boycott organisation on his breast in the location.

He was a short, wiry man and his eyes blinked owlishly behind the thick-lensed glasses he wore. He took them off, wiped the lenses nervously with his handkerchief, and replaced the glasses on the bridge of his wide, flat nose. He cleared his throat before speaking and then, in a surprisingly loud voice, said: 'Do not believe it, my brothers. It is not for our leaders to say we walk or ride before first asking the will of the people of the location. The men of the bus company must think our leaders are but children to be so easily swayed by their words. Pay no heed to what is written in the newspapers because it is the word of the white man.'

His words reassured them but there were a few, already tired of the long walk, who said that it was a good thing. 'The white man has seen that the black man is also a man of his word.' Now they would ride.

Jonathan was filled with doubt. Always he was with those who suffered without protest. Always he was with those without a voice. Always he was with those who had to bear the many pains. Always he was with those who were unwanted, and always they lost.

He had thought that the boycott would last only the first day. Then the people of the location, with their tired limbs, would once more ride the buses and their purpose would die. But when it entered the second day, the third day, and the day after that, his hopes mounted. Now, he began to hope that this would be the one time they would prove themselves men. It had become a symbol to him. As long as they walked, his life would not be altogether meaningless. He would be able to say with pride that he too was one of those who had walked the long walk when they proved to the bus company that they had a will of their own, and were not to be silenced into obedience by words.

Jonathan was depressed during his delivery round. When he read the newspapers his despair swamped him, and he felt cold in the afternoon sun. He felt betrayed. The paper stated that an agreement had been reached and that the following morning the buses would be filled. The boycott would be over.

To forget, he busied himself with his work and was relieved when he was given a stack of deliveries that would keep him occupied for the rest of the afternoon.

Work done, he joined the line of walkers ascending the first incline out of the city. They were a silent lot, and when someone asked if it was to be the last day of the long walk, they answered him with shrugged shoulders and heads shaken in bewilderment. The lines merged into one long column of heavy hearts and dragging feet. There were no jokes, no laughter. Only doubts and uncertainty. The ringing footsteps turned into drumbeats of defeat.

The walk was long and the road without end. The cars stopped and they looked without interest at those who climbed inside. They passed with apprehension the first group of grinning policemen. Their betrayal seemed complete when they were not stopped.

A youth raised his voice. 'Azikwelwa, my brothers and sisters.'

Those who had heard the youth's outburst turned their heads and stared at him and they buzzed with curiosity.

'Has news been heard?' 'Do we walk the long walk tomorrow?' 'What has happened?' they shouted, but there was no answer.

Then a voice cried, 'We will hear tonight in the location,' and it was taken up and passed along the ranks. The stride of the walkers seemed to lengthen, and Jonathan's heart kept pace with their footsteps.

They passed further blocks of policemen. No one was stopped or asked for a pass. The cars loaded with people passed unchallenged. The miles slipped behind them as they hurried to the location.

After supper, Jonathan walked with the others to the football field where the boycott organisation held its meetings and pushed himself to the front. The field filled. When he turned his head, he could no longer see where the field ended and the street began.

A speaker mounted an upended crate, hands held aloft. It was the same man who had spoken on the Square during the afternoon. His voice roared.

'The bus company has taken it upon itself, after speaking to those who could never speak for us, to have it printed in the papers of the white man that the boycott is ended! Is done with! That we have, like little children, agreed to their talks and will board the buses tomorrow. But they are wrong! This is our answer. Azikwelwa! Azikwelwa!. . .' The rest of the speech was lost in the clamour pouring from the open throats. And when other speakers tried to speak they met with the same result.

Again the backyards of the shebeen queens were flooded and skokiaan was to be had for the asking.

Jonathan sat on a bench with a mug of skokiaan untouched, a bemused smile on his face. A drinker opposite was slumped against the wall and his wife looked boldly at Jonathan. Looking at her, and the people swarming around him, Jonathan felt a surge of love sweeping through his body and he raised his mug to the woman.

'Azikwelwa, my sister!'

A Case of Guilt

He was on the way to the lavatory when a rattle jarred the front door. He glanced at his watch. Five fifteen. He wondered who it could be. Who would disturb them that early in the morning? The knocking was repeated with an urgency that compelled him towards the door.

'Dammit!' he murmured under his breath. 'Can't one even piss in peace?' He switched the stoep light on and unlocked the door. Two policemen confronted him. One held a brown form in his hand.

'Wilfred Kannemeyer?' He nodded his head, puzzled at their presence. 'I've got a warrant for your arrest.'

'Arrest? Why, what have I done?'

The policeman looked at the form before replying. 'The charge is non-payment of provincial tax for two years.'

'But that's wrong,' he stuttered. 'I paid the money last week. All of it! I've got the records to prove it.'

'That's got nothing to do with me. This warrant says you're under arrest.'

'But I've got the receipts at my office,' he tried to reason.

'Do you want us to take you in like this?' the other

policeman asked in a soft voice.

From the bedroom came the voice of his wife who had been roused by their words. He glanced over his shoulder then motioned to the policemen to come inside. One of them followed him down the passage to the bedroom and stationed himself on the threshold.

'What's wrong?' his wife asked in alarm.

'It's the police. I've got to go with them.'

'Why?'

'My tax. They say I haven't paid it.'

'But you paid it the other day.'

'I told them I've got the receipts at the office.'

The policeman looked at him pointedly to restrain their talk. He fumbled into his clothes then hurriedly kissed his wife on the cheek. 'Don't worry,' he told her, 'I'll phone you from the yard.'

He asked them as they walked down the short driveway whether he could go in his own truck.

'No! You can bloody-well get in the back of the van.'

His wife watched him through the living-room window as he climbed into the back of the van.

He could not see the streets they drove along and had to hold on to the seat that ran the length of the interior as the van slid around corners.

He tried to ease his mind. Despite their refusal to take him to his office and collect the receipts, everything would be cleared up at the charge office. These policemen were young and most probably from a country town. He had observed them taking note of the modernity of his lounge furniture; the coffin-like stereophonic sound system; the wall-to-wall carpeting and the electric clock ornamenting the shelf over the fireplace. The truck, almost filling the carport, was a late model, as was the Mini crouching alongside it. Yes, they'd resent a coloured man owning things beyond the reach of the meagre salaries they earned as policemen.

The van stopped with a jerk and he was jolted off his seat and sent sprawling. The door opened and he was ordered out.

A policeman stood sleepy-eyed behind the counter. 'Book him,' his escort said, flinging down the form.

Particulars entered, he was told to move to the other side of the counter. He realised that he was actually going to be locked up.

'It's all a mistake,' he blurted. 'I've got my . . . .'

His protest was ignored and he was hustled down a passage leading to the cells.

A cell was unlocked and he was thrust inside.

Three men wrapped in blankets occupied the cell. One of them raised his head at his entrance. 'Cigarette?' was the greeting. He searched his pockets, not sure if he had any. He found a packet and offered one to the man. A grunt was his thanks. He lit one for himself.

The floor was cement and the cell the size of a barn. A steel panel served as door, and a secondary door was barred. A wired window in the steel panel, closed on the outside, was fitted at about head-level. A wooden ledge, about a foot wide, ran lengthwise along a wall. The place had a cold and forbidding air. He was sobered by the sight of the three men wrapped in blankets, sleeping as if unconcerned by their surroundings.

I should've insisted on speaking to the sergeant in charge, he told himself.

Twice the door of the cell opened and a man was shoved inside.

Breakfast, later, consisted of two thick hunks of bread thinly smeared with jam, and a mug of coffee.

He gagged on the bread and hurriedly swallowed

the coffee to clear his throat. His companions seemed to have no difficulty finishing their breakfast.

They were ushered from the cell into the yard of the police station. The occupants from the other cells were also lined up, fourteen men in all.

At the command of one of the policemen they formed a line.

'I said ten to a line! Move, skollies, move!'

A shoving ensued and those at the end of the line sheepishly formed up in front. They acknowledged their names: some with grunts, others in bewilderment, and one or two with a cheerfulness which to him seemed unnatural.

They were left standing for about fifteen minutes, and before they broke rank they were again checked numerically.

The policemen were able to fit all of them into the small confines of the van. They were shoved in tight, the last two assisted by a kick in the rear.

He rehearsed his speech for the officer-in-charge in between trying to find space to breathe and adjusting to the shifts of the van.

The van stopped with its customary jerk but their numbers saved them from being slammed against the metal sides.

They lined up and were led inside the charge office where a form was handed over and signed. Then they were moved to the prison yard.

The prison yard was full. His apprehension increased as he scrutinised his fellow-prisoners. A few, like himself, showed their fear of the position they found themselves in. A handful of African workers, mainly middle-aged, stared perplexedly around. Almost all of them were dressed in working clothes.

Among them prowled the hyenas, howling their

cruel laughter as they sprang upon their victims, claiming a jacket, ripping off a belt, pulling off shoes forcibly, delivering slashing blows. He shrank from them and sought refuge in the toilet block.

Men stood around in small groups. Water from the taps seemed to have flooded the cement floor and the stench of urine and excrement was strong. Heads were raised at his entrance. He moved to one of the taps to avoid their questions.

His attention was attracted to a group in a corner as he bent over the tap. A whimper of pain fluttered to his side.

He could not make out at first who was suffering, as, apart from the whimpering, not a word was said. Then one of the men moved aside. He was confronted with a man, almost a youth, crouching with his trousers around his ankles and his shirt above his waist. Then his view was cut off again. Another of the men covered the naked buttocks and the whimpering resumed.

Dear God! he screamed silently. Isn't there anyone to put a stop to what they're doing?

The scene was nightmarish. The toilet block with its flooded floor — the interior shadowy, the groups of silent men casting surreptitious glances at the figures huddling over the crouched man in the corner; the only sound the whimpering coming from their midst.

His gall rose and he tightened his stomach muscles. He did not open the tap. Without looking at anyone, he stumbled back into the sunlit yard.

Avoiding the toilet block, he attached himself to a section of men who seemed of quieter mien. An African squatted next to him, his hands holding a parcel of sandwiches wrapped in brown paper.

'We going to work, many of us. Then the police

stop me. It was just my bad luck my papers was not with me. They throw me into the van. It always happens.' He pointed at the rest of the men who had been brought in with him. 'Every day some of us is pick up. There so many papers one must carry to show that one can walk in the city, and then there's always the dompass. If you forget that, they show you no mercy. They even pick you up in the location in the middle of the night if you go outside to relieve yourself and the dompass isn't in your pocket. We have no right in the country of our birth. Every move we make depend on the right piece of paper in our pocket. Life is heavy, very heavy, for us with the laws of the white man.'

He related what he had observed in the toilet block.

The man on the other side of him nudged his side and pointed cautiously at one of the hyenas dragging what appeared to be a youth into one of the cell blocks facing the yard.

'That's how they operate. If you go in for the first time, or you can't fight back, then they strip you of everything you got. Not that they would need it. They just take it because they consider it their right. And if you a young one then they make a woman out of you.'

The iron door enclosing the yard swung open and a coloured warder bawled out a string of names, stirring them into action.

Those whose names were called stepped through the gate. Those nearest to them urged in loud voices the messages to be relayed to their homes or places of employment.

The scene was re-enacted several times, and each time he hurried to the gate hoping that his name would be called. He felt that all hope was slowly being drained from him as, each time, the gate slammed shut. He had been arrested less than four hours. Already the outside world had forgotten that he existed.

The gate opened upon four convicts in faded khaki jackets and frayed shorts, each couple carting a heavy iron pot. Two more convicts followed with a huge wicker basket containing small dixies. A warder escorted them.

They were bawled into lines and made to pass between the two iron pots whose contents were ladled into a dixie and shoved at each man passing.

He looked at the congealing mass in the rust-speckled dixie. A large lump of mealie meal had been sprinkled with what looked like beans. He poked a finger at it and a sour smell emanated.

'Hell, my dog eats better than this,' he murmured softly as he sat with his back to the wall.

'Yes, dogs eat better than this,' his neighbour said in a matter-of-fact voice, 'but then, prison is not made for animals. We, when in prison, is less than the animals outside. If you mistreat a animal the law will take you. And when they get you, you treated worse than a animal. The thing is not to be caught.'

The words expressed his feelings and he felt bold enough to ask why his neighbour had found himself inside.

'I was on my way to work on the railways, minding my own business, smoking my morning pill, when they take me. I know they going to book me for being in possession of dagga. Fuck the law! My dagga smoking don't harm nobody.'

There was nothing he could say in commiseration. The smoking of dagga was heavily frowned upon in his circle. That was for skollies, and not respectable coloured people.

His neighbour eyed his sportsjacket and gaberdine trousers.

'Why they take you in? Fraud or receiving stolen property?'

He shook his head and blurted out his story.

His neighbour nodded his head in sympathy. 'Not to worry. You soon be out. You don't belong inside here. You pay your tax but those young, snot-nosed bastards have no other way to show that they boss.'

The words cheered him and he felt encouraged to ask whether he could be of any assistance to his neighbour.

'Hell, you don't know me. I know what's going to happen to me after I been in front of the old man. A straight six months. If luck is with me — after all it was only a pill — they give me a suspended sentence and a fine. My old lady will find the money and get me out of this shithouse.'

He looked at the yard filled with men; the cell blocks; the toilet block and the iron gate shutting them in. He made a decision.

'My name is Wilfred Kannemeyer. If it is as you say, and the magistrate will let me out, then I'll come back and pay your fine. You don't have to bother about paying me back.'

The gate clanged open but their rush was halted by six policemen.

'Come'n. Line up! Fifteen to a row.'

He kept close to his new-found friend. They were slapped and jerked into lines which conformed to the new specification. Then, after a roll-call, they were consigned to cells.

In the cell, three members of the hyena pack prowled among them. They closed in on him. 'What you in for?' one of them asked.

He glanced at his friend for support before answering.

'Oh, so you don't want to pay tax,' his interrogator said. 'We work and we pay tax.'

He was slapped in the face before he could reply. He staggered back, tear-stung.

The men around him moved away, leaving him in their custody.

'Look at the jacket he got on. Just my size.'

He was twirled around and the jacket wrenched off his shoulders before he could protest. He held on to the hem.

'You can't take my . . . .'

A blow stopped his protest and he doubled up in pain.

Not one of the others made any sign of protest at what had happened to him.

He was hoisted by the shirtfront and slapped several times across his face, each blow punctuated by a curse. His feet were kicked out from under him and he collapsed in a heap. A torn jacket was flung at him, covering his face.

Footsteps approached him and he cowered underneath the jacket, fearful of a kick. The jacket was removed and he looked up into the face of the man whose fine he had been prepared to pay.

His first reaction was that of anger. 'Why didn't you stop them? You know their tricks. Why did you let them beat me up like this?' He rubbed gently at a swelling on the side of his face. 'And I was going to pay your fine.'

'Nothing I can do about it.' There was no apology in the words. 'There's no way you can help yourself. If I climb in, all of them take me. I be worse off. You lucky they only take your jacket. You soon be out of here, and I be left with them. You don't have to pay my fine. I can work out my piece.'

A muffled scream came from the back of the cell as the hyenas trapped another victim. He looked at the faces of the other men. Most of them reflected their nervousness at what was happening. One or two giggled apprehensively. The few who looked capable of asserting themselves looked on unconcerned.

He realised that his friend was right. If one could not defend oneself, it was hopeless looking for aid from the others. Each was concerned only with his own safety.

'I'm sorry,' he said. 'I guess you're right. It's just that I can't get over it. They're just like animals. Don't they understand how it must be for all of us?'

His friend laughed cynically.

'Come here more times. You know what happen if you try that preaching line with them? They kick you from here to the remand yard. You be damn lucky you don't end up somebody's whore while inside.'

His mind scurried away hastily from the scene in the toilet block with the whimpering youth. His friend nodded his head to where the hyenas were amusing themselves forcing two of their victims to sing and dance.

'This is their land. When they inside, they boss. You must be less than animal to make out here.'

The cell door was unlocked and they all stared expectantly.

'Wilfred Kannemeyer!'

He looked at his friend, then moved towards the door.

'Out!' the warder said.

'You mean I can go. Won't I have to appear in

court?'

'No. The case has been withdrawn.'

He hesitated for a moment. I'm going out. They won't be able to touch me again. I'll lay a charge against them.

'They took my jacket.'

The warder entered the cell. 'Who?' he demanded, glaring at the inmates who stood with lowered eyes.

He confronted the man who had robbed him of his jacket.

'This one.'

'I didn't take it,' the man protested. 'He give it to me. Ask them,' pointing to those around him.

No one supported his plea.

The jacket was returned to him and his robber rewarded with a blow across the shoulder with a truncheon.

'Do you want to lay a charge?'

'Yes,' he replied, feeling that the prosecution following the charge would in some manner be retribution for all the agony suffered by the victims of the hyenas.

He assured his friend before leaving the cell that he would pay his fine.

The locking of the cell door, and the iron gate cutting off the yard: he felt it receding, the nightmare of men turned into beasts, where abnormality was the norm.

Caesar's Law

Outside, the wind whined strongly as it whipped through the trees, stripping the dead leaves. The priest stopped his perusal of the life of St. Augustine, and listened to the sound. He eased his fat posterior into a more comfortable position, stretched his legs and gave a soft sigh. Behind him, a heater sent rays of warmth through the room. There was a knock at the door: another interruption. He lowered the book he held and gave two deep, throat-clearing coughs before speaking.

'Come in. Come in.'

The door swung open and Johannes, who worked in the garden, stood on the threshold, cap deferentially doffed and held in horny hand.

'Someone to see you, Farder. A young woman.'

He looked searchingly at the brown face seamed with furrows and topped with a crop of tightly-curled tufts.

'Tell her to come inside, Johannes. And, thank you.'

The old man bobbed his head in acknowledgement and made a sign to the woman in the passage. He closed the door behind him and returned to the raking of leaves.

The priest took in the awkward movement of the young girl and the bulge her belly made which her loose-hanging coat could not conceal. He smiled encouragingly and extended a hand at the chair on the other side of the desk.

'Please take a seat.' His voice was soft and soothing. 'Now, what is it about?'

The girl did not reply, her fingers worrying the handkerchief balled in one hand. He noticed that her left hand lacked a wedding ring.

A faint rumbling of unease started in the pit of his stomach. He was a gentle man and all forms of violence — physical, spiritual and moral — distressed him. His younger years had been spent in ministering to the needs of parishioners gathered from the tenements huddled around his church. Their sometimes bloodied faces and battered bodies always made him feel limp, as if their pain had been inflicted upon himself, and when called in to act as peacemaker between two brawlers, he would send silent appeals aloft for help from his heavenly Father. At his age he had welcomed the prospect, when a transfer came his way, of a new and prosperous church among parishioners less familiar than his previous flock with the inside of a court-room.

'Speak up, my girl. No need to be shy. What's your name?'

'Hester Mathee.'

The priest scanned her face. 'I haven't seen you attending church, Hester. Are you a member of my parish?'

'No, Father.'

'To which church do you belong?'

'I don't belong to any church, Father.'

'Come now, my daughter. Surely you must belong

to a church? You must've been baptised and you're more than old enough to be confirmed.'

'I was baptised and confirmed in the Anglican church but I stopped going to church some time ago.'

The priest's voice took on a firmer tone.

'Have you lost faith, my daughter?'

'No, Father. I just stopped going.'

'You're not one of those young men and women, long-haired and in need of a bath, who have rejected the church because to them, with their permissiveness, the church has become too old-fashioned an institution? They've rejected all the beliefs they've been taught as children. They think their salvation lies in drug-taking.'

The girl lowered her head.

'And your parents, have they also stopped going to church?'

'My father is dead but my mother goes to church regularly.'

The priest shook his head reproachfully.

'A girl brought up in a church-going home, and yet you don't attend church. Do you think that you can go through life without God's help? Don't you feel the need for God?'

'I've stopped going to church, Father, but I haven't rejected God.'

'God is the church. You cannot accept Him and reject His house of worship. Which church does your mother attend?'

'She goes to St. Paul's in Woodstock.'

'Ah, Father Dawson's parish. We were ordained together in St. George's Cathedral. That was many years ago. The dreams we had when we were ordained! Our hopes were high. A diocesan. Oh well. It was the dream of youth. How is Father Dawson? Oh yes. You wouldn't know, not going to church. Where do you stay, Hester?'

'Walmer Estate, Father.'

'Were you baptised and confirmed in the same church?'

'Yes, Father.'

'Tell me, Hester. Why did you come here?'

'I want to get married, Father.'

'Then you should approach Father Dawson. Surely he'd be very pleased to see you married in the church where you were first introduced to the Glory of God and the mysteries of the church.'

'Father,' the rest of the words tumbled out, 'I'm going to have a baby.'

He laced his fingers across his stomach, then abruptly placed his hands on the desk. He knew what was going to follow. He had thought that, in his new parish, he had left behind the recurrent appearances of women big with child without the benefit of a marriage certificate.

'That's obvious. So, it's because you're going to give birth to a child that you're prepared to give the church a second chance. And you've come to me instead of Father Dawson. It seems that leaving the church has not altogether robbed you of shame.' The priest got up and moved around the desk to face the girl. 'This is where permissiveness has led you. You're going to give birth to a child innocent of your wilfulness. You've committed a grievous sin.'

The girl made as if to speak but was silenced by the priest's raised hand.

'Permissiveness leads to licentiousness and the moral decay of the mind. The church has made it quite clear that it will not condone the coupling of flesh between those who are not joined in marriage.'

'I love him, Father.'

'Better if you had shown the same love for the church. I feel sorry for your mother. She must be terribly disappointed by your action. Have you discussed it with her?'

'Yes, Father. She suggested I speak to Father Dawson.'

'Instead, you came to me. And the man who brought you into this sorry state, what are his intentions?'

'He wants to marry me. Would you marry us, Father?'

The slight rumblings in his stomach were placated by her words. She looks old enough. Perhaps it's one of the parents who have an objection, but this could be settled by a talk with all concerned.

'That's very commendable. I must praise him for his willingness to do his moral duty. And you, for taking the first step on the road to redemption. In my first parish, where I laboured for thirty-five years, my church was constantly filled with young women, pregnant and unwed, and their menfolk who refused to sanctify their misdeeds. And the unfortunate children entered the world as bastards. The law courts became an extension of my church, where I spent endless hours getting my parishioners out of jail and acting as peacemaker in their brawlings. It was a hard, and, at times, an unrewarding task. I'm grateful that I've been called to serve here. I can now look forward to a time of peace in the last years of my service to the church. This is the first time in three years that I've been approached by a woman unmarried and heavy with child. You understand, my daughter?'

'Then you'll marry us, Father?'

'As shepherd of my flock, it's my duty to bring an errant lamb back to the fold. You know, of course, that you've sinned,' — the voice again soft with just a coating of sternness — 'both of you. But I'm glad that you've come to see me.' His voice changed to the one he used when addressing the Mothers Guild preparing for their annual fete. 'I suppose you'd want to get married as soon as possible. Now, I think that it would be best done on a Wednesday evening. There'd be less people, as I feel certain that you'd want as little fuss as possible. Is the father a member of my parish?'

'No, Father.'

'Well, it doesn't really matter. The important thing is that he's willing to correct the wrong he has done. Why didn't you bring him along?'

'Father. There's one thing I have to tell you.'

'He's not a Catholic, is he?'

'No, Father. He's not a Catholic.'

'What is it then, my daughter?'

In a cold flat voice: 'I didn't bring him along because the father of my child is white!'

The rumblings in his stomach became a roar, erupting from his throat in the form of a loud gasp. His mind flashed back to his former parishioners. At least they had spared him this: the news that a white man was the cause of the pregnancy.

She looked at his shock and disbelief.

'Oh, my God!' The voice shaken.

'Yes, Father. He is white and we want to get married.'

'But you know . . . it's . . . it's . . . impossible,' he stammered. 'It's against the law.'

Ian had said the same thing. They had sat in the privacy of her bedroom, the door shut tight. They had sat in awkward silence, she avoiding his eyes. Then she spoke. 'Ian, I'm pregnant.' 'Are you sure?' 'Yes.' Silence built up between them and stretched, and she was filled with conflicting thoughts. Is this the end between the two of us? Is this child that I'm expecting going to be the thing that will tear us apart? Will he hate me for it? She heard him move and when she raised her head he was standing in front of her with hands extended. She stretched out her arms. Their hands clasped and her relief took the form of tears.

Ian waited until her weeping stopped. 'When did you find out?'

'Six weeks ago.'

'And all that time you've walked around with it, suffering Christ knows what tortures. My poor darling.'

Her lips were salty underneath his. 'You're not angry?'

'No, I'm not angry. Does your mother know?'

'No, I haven't told anyone.'

'We'll have to tell her. It's only right she should know. You know, of course, that we'll get married as soon as I can arrange for us to get out of the country. We'll go to Botswana, or Kenya. It should be easy for me to get a job teaching.'

'I won't go. You've only one more year to do then you'll have your arts degree. I won't allow you to drop out, not after all the struggle you went through to get where you are.'

'There's nothing we can do about it. The law won't allow us to get married.'

She had insisted that he was to complete his studies and that they were not going to leave South Africa. That she would find a way whereby they could get married. And that she would be the one to break the news to her mother.

'I know it's against the law, Father,' she said, her eyes on his, 'but I want you to marry us. It's not for myself I'm asking this. I know I've sinned, but must the sin be passed on to an unborn child?'

The priest could not hold her gaze and averted his eyes, searching for solace among the many framed texts adorning the walls. A gust of wind rattled the windows behind him and he shivered uncontrollably.

'What you ask of me is impossible, my child. The law has made it clear that there shall be no marriage ties between those who are white and those who are not. I cannot perform such a deed.'

'I know what the laws of the land state, Father. And I also know what the law of God states.'

Help me, Father. Why must this happen to me? Why couldn't she have gone to her own church? How can I do this thing she asks of me when she knows just as well as I what the consequences would be of breaking the law?

'Why did you come to me?'

'You are a man of God!'

The priest walked back to his desk and crumpled in his seat.

'You've told me of the women in your old parish who gave birth to bastard children. Do you want me to join them? Must I also give birth to a bastard?'

'I cannot do otherwise,' the priest said, closing his eyes to blot her out. 'The church does not make these laws. I cannot go against the laws of the land.'

'God has made no laws that forbid two people of different colour falling in love and wanting to have children. As you've said, Father, I've committed a mortal sin having a baby. Now, I want to wipe out that sin by getting married, and you refuse to help me rid myself of this sin. What sort of a man of God are you, Father?'

The priest cradled his head in his hands. The girl got up and moved to the side of the desk.

'Has the gift of love God gave us now become an unclean thing?'

'The Immorality Act,' the priest whispered meekly.

He could see it happening. Himself in the dock of a crowded court. The magistrate asking questions, questions he would have to answer truthfully, and each answer damning him in the eyes of the law. To be stripped of every dignity, his picture spread across the pages of the Sunday papers and tabloids. And, at the end of the trial, the sentence. He was sure he would be sentenced. Each successive couple charged under the Immorality Act was given a stiffer penalty. And, surely he would be sentenced to the maximum penalty, for it would be maintained that he, a priest, was inciting people to break the law of the land.

'Father. The Immorality Act is a man-made law that degrades all of us. Even you. The immorality is not of my doing. A marriage between my man and me could never be immoral in the eyes of God. It's written in the bible that man and woman should become as one in the eyes of God before they can bring children into the world. We want to follow the teachings of the bible. And Father, you are a man of God — who else could I come to? The law of the land says that there is to be no marriage, but what does the church say?'

'I cannot interfere in matters outside the church.'

'There were other priests, in other times, who were also afraid because of the laws of the land, but because their belief in the word of their God was stronger than their fear of the laws of the land, they were prepared to follow wherever God led. Even if to their death .... Father, I don't want you to die for me. I'm prepared to face God for what I've done. But would you be able to face Him after not doing what you should have done?'

The words from the holy book came to his mind. 'Render therefore unto Caesar the things which are Caesar's and unto God the things that are God's.' To follow the words of his Master to the letter would mean the end of a dream of peaceful old age, of heated vestries with glass-fronted bookcases, of security and comfort. He prayed silently. Dear Lord, please forgive me. I am weak.

'You've no right to say this to me.'

'But I have. You are my spiritual father, and every father desires the best for his daughter. Yet, you deny what's best for me as you now deny your heavenly father!'

'God help me,' the priest murmured brokenly.

'Father, you've seen black mothers and daughters nursing white children, giving them the same love they have for their own. Has this love now turned leprous when shared between a black woman and a white man? You've accused me of permissiveness but whose sin is worse? Was it too permissive of me to fall in love with one of another colour, or are you a priest who is not permissive enough to fulfil his priestly duties?'

'Why do you crucify me, my daughter?'

'No, Father. I'm the one being crucified. So is the child I'm carrying in my belly. I'm being crucified because you, Father, a man of God, will not follow the teachings you preach. As a child attending Sunday school, I was given the picture of Jesus surrounded by children of many colours and of all nations. I was told that Jesus had said that we are all equal, that we must love one another. What has happened to the love in your heart, Father?'

The girl resumed her seat and leaned across the desk.

'Father,' she said. 'Listen. I've got a plan. We could come here one evening when you haven't any people coming, and you could marry us. You could lock the church. Marry us in your study. There'd be no need to place our names on your register. No one would know.'

He brushed his hand across his face. What she had said offered a way out. No one need know. He could do it after all the church affairs were completed for the evening. It would not take long. A few lines read, their vows said. Then, at the end of the ceremony, he would pronounce the words that would make them husband and wife, and their child would be born within Grace. No! No! he quaked.

'No. I cannot do it!'

'Cannot, or afraid to? What kind of a priest are you? They say that God is love, and you are a man of God.'

'Don't ask it of me, my daughter.'

'They were right. My mother and him. They said I wouldn't be able to find a priest with the guts to marry us.'

'I am a shepherd.'

When he raised his head he stared into her scorn-filled eyes.

'You're a miserable man! You have no right to wear the vestments of a priest! Your fear of the law-makers has made you party to making God's message of love a lie. It is you who should leave the church! You profane God's house with your hypocritical sermonising!'

'No! No!' His voice a wail.

The girl got up with an abrupt movement, almost knocking over the chair.

'What are you going to do, my daughter?'

'Nothing, man of God.' Her voice as bleak as sleet. 'Nothing, except wait out my time and give birth to my bastard child!'

She slammed the door on the priest and his conscience.

Johannes, leaves swirling around his feet, watched her as she walked down the short drive towards the gate.

The Party

The room was a large one, larger than any of the
rooms in the houses he had been in previously. He
scaled it mentally, comparing it with his own home.
Their two tiny bedrooms and dining-living room
would take up half of it, leaving space for the kitchen
and small yard. One wall was covered with a tapestry
and paintings, there were gilt-framed mirrors on the
others. Exploring one corner, he almost knocked an
ivory carving from its pedestal. The carpet underneath
his feet was as soft and lush as a municipal lawn.

Large as the room was, it could not contain the
many people crowding it, and they spilled into the
passage leading off it to the other rooms.

He gave what he hoped was a polite smile as the
woman squeezed into the small space left on the
couch. He could feel her thigh pressing warmly against
his own. He wanted to edge his leg away but that
would have been too obvious, so he shifted his
haunches to raise himself. She turned to him and
smiled.

'Don't get up, please. I know it's a bit of a jam, but
we should be able to manage.'

He shifted his body so that she would have a little

more space. 'It's my fault,' he said, 'I'm taking up too
much room.'

'It's kind of you to say that, but I'm afraid it's my
fault, really.' She smiled as she patted her hip.

He nodded his head as if to assure her that he also
had his troubles with a body that was not always
what he would have liked it to be, and to show that
he sympathised with her.

'Quite a crowd,' she said.

'Yes,' he replied.

'I wonder what has happened to the drinks? Have
you been served?'

'No.'

'Hold on to my seat and I'll see what I can do
about it.'

She was soon lost in the throng of bodies.

He changed his position so that his back rested
against the angle formed by the arm of the couch,
and spread his legs so that they covered the area
between his neighbour and himself.

He looked at the many people in the room. There
were a lot of women, outnumbering the men, and
they were all white. Of the men, there were only four
that were not white — himself and three others. The
other three he knew well. Of the whites, he knew no
one.

He was a stranger among strangers, and although
they spoke the same tongue, because of his colour he
felt deserted in an alien land.

He gazed around the room for his three friends and
the assurance they would give him. He spotted one,
before the swelling lines of bodies engulfed him. He
had a brief glance of another. Then a tightly-packed
group at the far end of the room attracted his attention. They parted to make way for a line of loud,

gesticulating women who wiggled their way across the room like conga dancers on a cinema screen. He saw Ron before the group reformed, glass in one hand, the other pointing into the air emphasising a point, self-assured. Then the gap was closed and he could only see backs.

He did not know what the topic was, but he knew that Ron would dominate the conversation. He envied Ron his calm, cool manner, his ability to mix without restraining thoug'its about colour, to bridge the gap as if there was none at all — or as if it did not apply to him, if a gap did indeed exist. His envy was without malice, and he hoped that with the passing of time he would also acquire that smoothness of manner, and be forever rid of the unease he felt now.

The room was loud with talk, but he could not separate the individual voices. The gruffer tones of the men merged with the shriller notes of the women, and, above the roar, like clanging cymbals, he could hear their laughter. Snatches of conversation came to him like so many broadcasts from different stations, their only link the degree of noise.

'Jack has done it again!' The announcement was greeted with laughter. 'By now one would think that he would have more sense.

He wondered who Jack was, and what he had done.

'Are you going to Margo on Friday evening?'

'Yes, darling.'

'Who will she have on show this time?'

'God alone knows! But if one is to judge by her previous dinners, it will be another genius of whose talent only Margo is aware. Are you going?'

'No, thanks. I'm not so hard up for a meal.'

His misgivings returned. Was this what he was up against? How could he deal with them? In this jungle of polished manners and sharp tongues he would be defenceless — a black sacrificial lamb.

Ron had insisted that he go with them. The party was to celebrate the publication of a book, the author's third. Critics thought it important.

He had become a supporter of the author when the first book was published, reading everything he wrote. He had at first backed out when told by Ron that a meeting could be arranged, but the invitation, or rather Ron, changed his mind.

'Look, William. I went to a lot of trouble to get you an invitation to the party so that you can meet Colin Ashworth. It's about time you started meeting people and going places,' Ron had said.

He flushed when he thought of the meeting fifteen minutes earlier.

'Colin. This is William Apollis. He swears by you as a writer,' Ron said, introducing him. He stiffly poked out a hand to meet that of a white man a head taller than himself. 'How do you do?' he said, hating himself for uttering the conversational inanity.

'So this is the William you've told me about.' Turning to him, the white man continued: 'I hear you also write, William. Would you let me have a look at some of your stuff, soon?'

He looked into a pair of understanding eyes. A choking heat filled him. 'Yes . . . yes,' he stammered.

'Excuse me for a moment.' Their host had left them to greet a couple entering.

Ron called greetings to several people as they crossed the room, stopping to speak to some of them before passing on. William got separated from the others during their progress and made for the couch.

A tray was held before him, and as he reached for a glass filled with sherry, he caught a glimpse of a bare bosom. He could not help looking at the breasts so temptingly displayed. The woman moved towards the next person, unaware of the havoc aroused within him.

He looked at the women in their form-fitting dresses with low necklines, and again he had the feeling that they should have been on a cinema screen. Their movements gave him a three-dimensional effect from where he sat, their chatter providing the script for the scene.

Immersed in the idea, he forgot the people seated next to him and concentrated on the changing pattern. His eyes focused on a particular person, lost him, then found him again. A woman attracted him. She was not young, but she had a bearing that compensated for her lost youth. She could only play the part of a queen or a duchess. The game delighted him and he followed it in earnest, counting how many times he could pick her out before finally losing her.

He was aware that someone was looking at him, and guiltily raised his head like a little boy caught peeping at forbidden things.

It was the woman who had offered to get him a drink. She had a tray on which were balanced a plate filled with snacks, a bowl of mixed nuts and two glasses of gin and lime. He jumped to his feet.

'Please, sit down,' she said after seating herself, shifting her body so that he could fit in. He sank down beside her.

'I've brought something to nibble at. I don't think you've had anything to eat since you came. I see you have a drink, at least. Oh, well! You can have this one too.'

'No, thank you.'

'Do have it,' she urged him. 'Besides, I've been here longer than you.'

He took the second drink, carefully placing his empty glass at the side of the tray.

'What do you do?'

The friendliness of her smile soothed his panic.

'I write,' he said. 'At least, I try.'

'Have you had anything published?'

'Five.' Then he stopped, dismayed at his schoolboy eagerness.

'Where were they published?' she prompted him.

'They were all published locally, except for one — 'The Flower Seller' — which was published in London.'

'Wait a minute! I think I've read it. Yes, I have. It was in Argosy wasn't it? I loved it. So you are William Apollis.' A glow of warmth swept over him. 'You also wrote 'The Char's Birthday Wish' and 'The Golden Penny'. I always thought that those stories were not written by white writers. They were too authentic, too close to the subject.' She touched him lightly on the shoulder. 'You know what I mean. I must say it's a pleasure meeting you after enjoying your stories so much.'

She held out her hand. 'I'm Margo Pearce.' He gingerly wrapped his hand around her soft one. He wondered whether she was the same Margo who invited the dullest people to her dinners. As if to confirm it, she said, 'You must come to dinner and a drink at my place. Then we can really have a talk. There are some people I'd like you to meet.' She mentioned a few names — writers, artists, a sculptor — people Ron had told him about. Not well-known names, but all considered as sure to make their mark.

He burst out laughing. He could not help himself as he thought of the two women and their conversation.

How wrong both of them must be! If the people mentioned were dull, then the company those two moved in must be the wittiest and most talented in the land.

She looked at him, puzzled. 'Is it so funny, my asking you to dinner?'

'No, it's not that. I just thought of something I heard someone say just now.' All the time he was telling himself that it had its funny side. Dinner in a big house. He imagined how it would be, at a long table covered with a stiffly starched white cloth on which would be placed an array of knives and forks. At home, his mother always served dinner in the kitchen. The only time they ate in the dining room was on religious holidays.

'When would you be able to come? Would next Friday do? I could arrange for someone to pick you up or, if you prefer, you could come out by bus. I'm at Three Anchor Bay, St. John's Road. You can't miss it. It's a small house with a block of flats on each side.'

He searched for an excuse.

There was a difference between a party like this and a dinner. Here, there was the safety of numbers. He could withdraw into himself and be lost in the shuffle, but a dinner party would be more intimate. Would he do the right things? What if he should choose the wrong spoon or fork? Would they laugh at the blunder or would they ignore it and try to cover it with their talk? Both ways would be painful to him. It would be better to refuse.

He was undecided. He very much wanted to be in the presence of the people she had mentioned; he felt the need to mix with those who had the same yearnings as himself. Ron waved at him from across the room before being swept up into another group. He felt reassured. He would go.

'It would be less bother if I come out by bus.'

'It's no bother, William.'

'I'm sure I'd be able to find the place on my own, ma'am.'

'I shall be very angry if you don't call me Margo. Everyone else does.'

He rolled her name on his tongue a few times, savouring it before uttering: 'Margo.'

'Margo, dear. I don't think I've been introduced to your friend.'

He looked at a tall, slender young man; a study in black and white. His dark hair brushed flat on the skull contrasted sharply with his pale face. His eyes matched his hair, and above them his eyebrows were two streaks of black. He was dressed in a black suit with a white shirt and pencil-slim black tie.

'Oh, it's you, Edward. Meet William Apollis. He's going to be a first-rate writer. Remember, I'm the one who told you.' She turned towards him. 'William, this is Edward Blakely.'

Both name and face were familiar. Then he remembered. Blakely was a member of the Liberal Party or Congress of Democrats, he was not sure which. Again he felt that awkwardness when he shook hands.

'William is coming to dinner next Friday. You *are* still coming, aren't you?'

'Of course, Margo.' Then he turned to William. 'Would you excuse us for a moment? There are some people who want to meet Margo.'

'Not at all.' He felt bold enough to add, 'Then I'll see you next Friday, Margo.'

'Yes, and do bring some of your work.'

They were absorbed by the crowd.

He leaned back breathing deeply. The bustling scene — was he to be part of it? Would he be able to fit in freely without the constant inner fear that perhaps he did not belong? Would she have asked him to dinner if he were not the writer of the stories she enjoyed so much? What would her reaction have been if he had told her otherwise? That he was as nondescript as he looked, that he came mainly through Ron's urging?

The doubts awoke other thoughts he had tried to bury. These people, Ron had said, made no fuss about the colour of one's skin, accepted one for what one was, but were they really so open and casual? Or was it a pose they all assumed?

'Do you intend sitting on this couch for the rest of the evening?' Ron stood in front of him. 'What has happened to Margo? I saw you speaking to her a little while ago.'

'She left with another chap, Edward Blakely, who said that there were some people who wanted to meet her.'

'Oh, Edward. Looking like a corpse as usual, with his pale face and black eyes. What do you think of Margo?'

'She seems to be quite nice. She has . . . .'

'Yes, I know. She has invited you to dinner. She fancies herself a patron of the arts. She should've lived in the eighteenth century — then she could have turned her house into a salon. At least, you're making progress. It's about time that you crawled out of your shell. It's at parties like this that you'll meet people, important people who can really help you a lot if you go about it in the right way.'

He made no reply, silently wondering what the right way was.

Recalling Ron's attitude nine months before, he was not altogether sure whether he should be grateful

now. He had had his first story published. Previously
Ron had scarcely spoken a dozen words to him,
including him among those tolerated but never asked
to meet the white friends of whom Ron spoke so
intimately and whose names were often featured on
the social pages of the local newspapers. The few
times Ron had spoken to him, he had repeatedly
pointed out William's lack of feeling for art in any
form.

His story had brought about a change.

'I've read your story,' Ron had said. 'It's not a bad
effort. Is it your first?'

'No, it's not,' he replied. 'I've written several but
it's the first one to be published.'

'Why all the secrecy? Why didn't you tell me you
were interested in creative writing? There are some
chaps I could've introduced you to. Established
writers.'

The publication of a second and then a third story
made him a member of the select few Ron favoured.
'Come along with us tomorrow evening. Tom Hopkirk
is having a party at his place in Devil's Peak.'

'No,' he had replied. During the following months
Ron's invitations had become more insistent, but he
had refused them all. The picture of himself mixing
socially with whites filled him with dread. The whites
at work smiled at him and spoke to him, then forgot
him, remembering him only when they wanted something done.

Ron spoke of the parties he had been to and the
people he had met, and gradually his resistance
weakened and the yearning to meet and become part
of the world Ron described became stronger. He could
not hold out any longer when Ron told him about the
invitation from Colin Ashworth. He accepted.

'Let's join the others,' Ron said now.

'No. I'll sit here a little while longer. Perhaps Margo will come back. I'd like to continue our talk.'

He was pathetically grateful for the friendliness of Margo and the understanding shown by Colin Ashworth. Ron looked at him with raised eyebrows, then left him. Another woman sank down beside him. It was the woman he had decided to cast as a duchess. She gazed at him as if he were a curio. She should have had a lorgnette, he thought. Then she spoke. 'Tell me, what do you do?' Her voice cold and condescending.

Her tone and manner chilled him, and he felt an instant dislike.

'Do?'

'Yes!'

'I work in an office. I'm a . . .' — he thought of making himself a clerk — '. . . I'm a messenger.'

'I don't mean your occupation.' She waved that aside as if it were a distasteful object. 'Do you paint or write? If I like what you do, I can very helpful.'

'No.'

'Come now. I bet that isn't true. The others do either one or the other.'

There was no need to ask who 'the others' were. She must obviously be one of the important people Ron had told him about.

'I've told you the truth. I don't do a thing.' He was not worried about deceiving her. If she were to check with Ron it would be just too bad. She was not going to add him to her collection.

'You don't paint and you don't write and you are a messenger?' Her eyes and voice jabbed at him.

'That's right.'

'Then what are you doing here?'

'Same as you.' His dislike for her strengthened him,

overcoming his trembling. 'I'm here because I was invited.'

'I don't want any of your damn cheek!' Her voice jumped several octaves. People seated on the couch and those nearby turned to stare. She got up, nostrils flaring and breath drawn in audible snorts. A horrified Ron pushed his way towards them.

'Mrs Meredith, what is the matter?' Ron exclaimed. 'What has happened?'

'I have been insulted by this impertinent messenger boy!' she said, pointing an accusing finger at William.

Ron faced him. 'Get up and apologise at once!' he said, his voice thick with reproach.

William looked at Ron whose composure was crumbling with the effort to placate Mrs Meredith. He was sick to the stomach at what he considered a betrayal on Ron's part, and his former unease gave way to anger. She would have accepted him if he had told her that he, too, was a writer, and here was Ron, without hearing his side of it, taking her part. His admiration for Ron turned to contempt. He knew why Ron had been so ingratiating. His talents, and those of 'the others', were on display like virgins to be sold to those like her, and Ron was their pimp.

It was for this, to walk in the shadow of a Mrs Meredith, that Ron had snubbed his own kind, pushed them aside, forgetting that he too came from them. And this was what he had envied Ron for: the ability to converse and move with ease among these patrons, and provide virgin talents for their inspection. His anger brought a rush of blood to his head, making speech impossible as he glared at Ron. He got up from the couch and blindly pushed his way through the animated throng, unaware of the approval evident in Margo Pearce's eyes.

The Sacrifice

He sat on the roof, his back against the outside wall of the room he shared with three younger brothers and a smaller sister. The sun warmed him pleasantly and he wriggled his toes in gratification.

In front of him were a sloping shelf of roofs and a vista of small yards hidden under garlands of multi-coloured washing hanging from criss-crossed lines.

A black and white cat was also taking the sun. Its lean lines showed that it was not a spoiled parlour cat but a hunter of the alleys and rooftops.

He looked at the pigeon-loft on the roof, reached out for a fragment of plaster fallen from the walls after the rains and pitched it at the cat.

The plaster spattered to pieces and a blur of movement transformed the slumberer into an alert prowler. Another piece of plaster spattering at its feet sent the cat scattering with small, graceful bounds, clearing the space between two roofs with disdainful ease.

Above his head, the birds released from their cote wheeled and banked, flying in a compact mass then breaking apart, their winged bodies showing glittering silver patches in the sun's light.

His spirit soared with the birds as they crossed his vision. They joined other flocks of birds from lofts on the surrounding roofs, only to break apart and re-form as a distinct group. From inside the loft came the cooing of birds huddled over their eggs, and the chirping of their young, the small, soft bodies covered with down.

His eyes strove to hold a particular bird, then lost it in the blur of wings. His uncle had often told him, before he died, that after death he would like to reappear on earth in the shape of a bird. The two of them had laughed at that together and speculated as to which species his uncle would choose. He had plumped for an eagle, excited by the thought that his uncle would be able to travel the world's winds, proud and aloof from all the other birds.

His uncle had waited until he ran out of breath and words, face flushed and animated. Then he had told him softly that he would prefer to return as a pigeon, or a skolly duif as they termed their birds, most of which he and his uncle patiently trapped with loose mealies attached to a string on Sunday afternoons in the square deserted of cars.

They had buried his uncle the day before. For two evenings his uncle had lain in the front room down-stairs. The room could not contain all the mourners who came. He had not realised that his uncle knew all those people who came to look at him stiffened and dead in his coffin.

Then yesterday. The line of cars with the hearse in front of the house. There was even a bus. He would have liked to have joined the rest of the youngsters as they scrambled about the upper deck and sat with their noses pressed flat against the windows.

At the cemetery the people piled up behind the

pall-bearers and passed through the gate. Huge pine trees, their tops higher than the telephone poles, were silent sentries on each side of the path.

Their feet stumbled on the loose pebbles as they walked. He wondered who collected the hundreds of shattered dry pine cones strewn on the ground. A fresh offering showered down as the wind sighed its sympathy. He cleared his throat to ask his mother whether he could gather some but was alarmed by the set faces around him and the measured tread of their feet.

In silence he walked along with them.

Preceding the coffin, the priest chanted: 'I am the resurrection and the Life, said the Lord! He that believeth in Me, though he were dead, yet shall he live, and whosoever liveth and believeth in Me shall never die.'

Paths, like roads, branched out from the main one, leading to rows of mounds.

Death held no terrors for him. The first time it happened, he was too young to understand and was bewildered by the tears of his mother and father. But now he accepted it. People grew old and died or they got sick and the same thing happened.

Like his uncle. Brown and tall. Taller than his father and most of the men he knew. His uncle had been like one of the trees he passed. Then all at once he was felled. He lay stretched out under his blankets, sweat covering his face and body. When he spoke, his voice was without substance, issuing from a hollowed hulk.

When death closed his uncle's eyes, he wept. His tears were not caused by the fear of death which filled his mother and father and those who came to see his uncle as he lay stretched in his white, starched shirt waiting for his coffin.

The shuffle of feet could not muffle the chanting of the priest: 'I know that my Redeemer liveth, and that He shall stand at the latter day upon the earth. And though after my skin worms destroy this body, yet in my flesh I shall see God; Whom I shall see for myself, and mine eyes shall behold, and not another.'

Then the open grave was before them and the lone voice was replaced by others joining in the hymn.

The grave filled, the priest took up his chanting. 'Glory be to the Father, and to the Son and the Holy Ghost; as it was in the beginning, and ever shall be, world without end. Amen.'

He asked himself whether his uncle would have tolerated their chanting. He had always been closer to his uncle than to his father. His uncle, usually gentle in speech, had a sharp tongue when dealing with hypocrisy. Now, his own mind cried out in protest against the service. The ritual seemed to him to be another indignity thrust upon the mute body.

He wanted to be away from the people with their tears and hymns and prayers; away from the cemetery with its forests of tombstones, china flowers under glass, silent cherubs, madonnas with outspread arms and chipped faces; away from the heaped mounds and the dry red gravel paths. He wanted to be away from them all, to be back home, on the roof with the pigeons, to communicate his grief to them.

He found himself next to his mother as they walked to the cars parked outside the cemetery. She took hold of his arm and turned a tear-stained face to him.

'Now, he's gone too.'

For her, when the grave had swallowed her brother's body it was the final act of withdrawal. For her son, it was different. He stared at the sky, at the wild birds wheeling overhead. As long as he could see a winged creature, his uncle would be with him. He writhed underneath her touch and she mistook the movement for his understanding of her grief.

The mourners, with their commiserating words, departed after they had finished their funeral tea and biscuits.

He felt that the birds had sensed how things had changed. When he fed them, they swirled around his head, darting from side to side and flitting towards the window through which he had climbed on to the roof, as if waiting for his uncle to appear.

He spoke to the birds softly: 'He's not here any more. He's gone. But he'll be coming back one of these days. He told me so. Just you wait and see. One of these days there'll be a new bird waiting for you. It will be the biggest bird you've ever seen. Even bigger than you, Pop-eye.' He pointed a finger at a puffed up bird which had lost an eye in a tussle with a marauding cat.

As he sat, he hopefully scanned the sky for a sign of the big bird that was to manifest his uncle's re-appearance. Deep inside of him he knew that it was not possible, but he could not rid himself of his forlorn hope.

His father and his teacher had often rebuked him for what they termed day-dreaming. They did not realise that his land of fantasy was more real to him than the dreary classroom with its stifling closeness.

Through the open window he could hear his mother and father conversing in the kitchen, the gruff voice of his father dominating the conversation.

He had wandered forlornly in and out of the sick-room. Once, when his uncle was awake, he had ventured to speak.

'Uncle Jonas,' he faltered, 'what's going to happen to the birds?'

His uncle did not have the strength to reply. He stared helplessly at the sweat-covered face. His mother entered the room at that moment and he turned to her with his plea.

She nudged him gently from the room.

'Don't bother your Uncle Jonas. I'll give you the money.'

He did not bother to enquire where she would get the money from when she was always complaining that they never had sufficient money in the house.

Feeding the pigeons, he spoke to them softly, as he always did, adding a larger portion of feed to his favourites.

'Come'n, my beauties. Eat. Everything is going to be all right. I'm going to look after you. I'll see that you don't starve.'

He placed a kernel of grain between his lips and a pie-coloured pigeon, pouting its breast ridiculously, flipped on to his wrist which he had raised to the level of his mouth and pecked at the grain.

'I know it costs money,' he overheard his mother say softly, 'but what are we going to do? Sell them to someone?'

He held his breath. His heart was in his father's keeping. To be parted from his pigeons now, with the death of his uncle still an open wound, would be unbearable. Birds he had cared for from the moment they had emerged from the egg, naked of feather, and fragile. Were they now to be taken away from him and given to another? His mouth formed words of protest that only he could hear.

'What are we going to do about the birds?' his father asked.

'Can't we keep them?' his mother replied, 'Jonas would've wanted us to.'

'And who's going to look after them, clear up the mess they make?'

'Willieboy will. As he always does. You know he's the one who helped Jonas look after his birds.'

'Yes, that's why I could never get him to do anything for me! He's always too busy with the damn birds!'

He had no way of telling his father that his gruff voice and abrupt manner made him recoil in apprehension, forcing him to seek in his mother's brother the understanding his father should have accorded him.

'Why is it that papa never joins us?' he had once asked his uncle. 'And why is he always angry when he speaks to me?'

'Your papa isn't angry with you. It's just that he works so hard. And, like most of us, has nothing to show for it. Yes,' his uncle added softly, 'he should join us with the birds. It would bring him peace.'

The last part was beyond his understanding, and he placed it with the things grown-ups speak about when together.

Again his father's voice thundered angrily: 'What about their feed? Who do you think is going to pay for it? Do you know how much a week it costs?'

He could have told his father. It was his job every Saturday morning to go to the pet shop and buy the bag of mixed seeds. His uncle would give him the money. The Saturday before his uncle's death was the first time there had been no money.

His father spoke again: 'Who would buy them? It would be a different thing if they were prize birds. Skolly birds! What would you get for them?'

He let out his breath slowly.

'No. After all the money Jonas wasted on feeding

them, it's their turn to feed us. I'll kill us a potful for
Sunday. If we can't have chicken then we can have
them. They're smaller, but if you use curry, they'll
taste almost the same.'

His heart was a lump of ice spreading its chill
through his body.

He could see them stretched out in a row, their
necks twisted and their wings clipped. His father's
grinning face as he dipped the birds, one after the
other, into a basin of hot water to rid them of their
feathers. Then, when naked of their covering, their
bodies tiny and defenceless, they'd be popped into a
steaming pot. He could not think any further. His
stomach revolted and he retched convulsively. He
wiped his mouth with his sleeve.

I won't let them do it! he told himself fiercely. For
an instant, he thought of chasing the birds away, then
he realised that they would return to the loft after
circling the roof a few times. I'll kill them myself,
that's what I'll do! He thought of a way of doing it so
that the birds would not fall victim to his father's
appetite. I'll burn them! Yes. Burn them!

The thought sobered him. He walked down the
stairs making sufficient noise to warn his parents of
his approach.

'Do you think he heard?' his mother whispered.

'What does it matter!' his father said roughly. Then
to him: 'I'm going to kill the birds! We don't have the
money to keep them in feed! Do you understand?'

'Yes, father. We're going to have them for dinner
on Sunday.'

As he walked through the kitchen his father called
after him: 'Where are you going?'

'I'm getting the bag. It's time for their feed.'

The bag of feed in his hand, he hunted for the

bottle of paraffin his mother used for the lamps and the small pressure stove. When he found it he placed it in the bag and covered it with the mixed seeds.

No one spoke as he walked past his parents. When he gained the roof he heard their voices again but now they were indistinct.

He placed the bottle next to one of the loft supports and shook the bag of feed, pursing his lips and making cooing sounds. The birds recognised their feeding signal and swooped down, some of them landing on parts of his body.

He dipped both of his hands into the bag and withdrew them cupped and filled with seeds. The birds darted around his offerings.

'Goodbye, my beauties,' he whispered, 'They're not going to do it to you!'

He ushered them into their cotes, tossed handfuls of seed into the loft, and closed it with its fine mesh wire covering.

Tears streaming down his cheeks, he emptied the bottle of paraffin over the loft and took a box of matches from his pocket.

He struck one and held it to the stream of paraffin. Flaming tongues licked greedily at the dry wood soaked with oil. A spiral of smoke floated skywards. The trapped birds cooed their panic loudly, some of them beating their wings against the now-hot wire in an attempt to escape.

'Uncle Jonas,' he said between sobs as the flames consumed the loft, 'forgive me, please! I couldn't let them be eaten!'

Behind him, he could hear the alarmed cries of his father and mother.

The Park

He looked longingly at the children on the other side
of the railings: the children sliding down the chute,
landing with feet astride on the bouncy lawn; screaming as they almost touched the sky with each upward
curve of their swings; shrieking their demented joy at
each dip of the merry-go-round. He looked at them
and his body trembled and ached to share their joy.
Next to him, on the ground, was a bundle of clothing,
washed and ironed, wrapped in a sheet.

Five small boys, pursued by two bigger ones, ran
past, ignoring him. One of the bigger boys stopped.
'What are you looking at, you brown ape?' the boy
said, stooping to pick up a lump of clay. He recognised
him. The boy had been present the day he was put
out of the park. The boy pitched the lump, shattering
it on the rail above his head, and the fragments fell on
his face.

He spat out the particles of clay clinging to the
lining of his lips, eyes searching for an object to
throw at the boys separated from him by the railings.
More boys joined the one in front of him and he was
frightened by their number.

Without a word he shook his bundle free of clay,

raised it to his head and walked away.

As he walked he recalled his last visit to the park. Without hesitation he had gone through the gates and got on to the nearest swing. Even now he could feel that pleasurable thrill that travelled the length of his body as he rocketed himself higher, higher, until he felt that the swing would upend him when it reached its peak. Almost leisurely he had allowed it to come to a halt like a pendulum shortening its stroke, and then he had run towards the see-saw. A white boy, about his own age, was seated opposite him. Accordion-like their legs folded and unfolded in turn to send the see-saw jerking from the indentations it pounded in the grass. A hand pressed on his shoulder. He turned around to look into the face of the attendant.

'Get off!'

The skin tightened between his eyes. Why must I get off? What have I done? He held on, hands clamped on to the iron bar attached to the wooden see-saw. The white boy jumped off from the other end and stood there a detached spectator.

'You must get off!' The attendant spoke in a low voice so that it would not carry to the people who were gathering. 'The council say,' he continued, 'that us blacks don't use the same swings as the whites. You must use the swings where you stay.' His voice apologised for the uniform he wore, which gave him the right to watch over little white boys and girls and ensure they were not hurt while playing.

'There no park where I stay.' He waved a hand in the direction of a block of flats. 'Park on the other side of town but I don't know where.' He walked past them. The mothers with their babies, pink and belching, cradled in their arms, the children lolling on the grass, his companion from the see-saw, the nurse girls

— their uniforms their badge of indemnity — pushing prams. Beside him walked the attendant.

The attendant pointed an accusing finger at a notice board near the entrance. 'There. You can read for yourself.' Absolving himself from all blame.

He struggled with the red letters on the white background. 'Blankes Alleen. Whites Only.' He walked through the gates and behind him the swings screeched, the see-saw rattled, and the merry-go-round rumbled.

He walked past the park each time he delivered the washing, eyes wistfully taking in the scene.

He shifted the bundle to a more comfortable position, easing the pain biting into his shoulder muscles. What harm would I be doing if I were to use the swings? Would it stop the swings from swinging? Would the chute collapse? The bundle pressed deeper and the pain became an even line across his shoulders, and he had no answer to his reasoning.

The park itself, with its wide lawns and flower beds and rockeries and dwarf trees, meant nothing to him. It was the gaily painted red-and-green tubing, the silver chains and brown boards, his transport to never-never land, which gripped him.

Only once, long ago, and then almost as if by mistake, had he played on something to beat it. He had been taken by his father, one of the rare times he was taken anywhere, to a fairground. He had stood captivated by the wooden horses with their gilded reins and scarlet saddles dipping in time to the music as they whirled by.

For a brief moment he was astride one. He prayed it would last forever, but the moment lasted only the time it took him to whisper the prayer. Then he was standing clutching his father's trousers, watching the others astride the dipping horses.

Another shift of the bundle and he was at the house where he delivered the clothing his mother had washed in a round tub filled with boiling water, the steam covering her face with a film of sweat. Her voice, when she spoke, was as soft and clinging as the steam enveloping her.

He pushed the gate open and walked around the back, watching for the aged lap dog which at his entry would rush out to wheeze asthmatically around his feet and nip with blunt teeth at his ankles.

A round-faced African girl, her blackness heightened by the white starched uniform she wore, opened the kitchen door to let him in. She cleared the table and he placed the bundle on it.

'I call madam,' she said, the words spaced and highly-pitched as if she had some difficulty in uttering the syllables in English. Her buttocks bounced beneath the tight uniform and the backs of her calves shone with fat.

'Are you sure you've brought everything?' was the greeting he received each time he brought the bundle, and each time she checked every item and as usual nothing was missing. He looked at her and lowered his eyes as he said, 'Everything there, merrum.'

What followed had become a routine between the three of them.

'Have you had anything to eat?' she asked him.

He shook his head.

'Well, we can't let you go off like that.' Turning to the African woman in the white, starched uniform. 'What have we got?'

The maid swung open the refrigerator door and took out a plate of food. She placed it on the table and set a glass of milk next to it.

The white woman left the kitchen when he was

seated and he was alone with the maid. His nervousness left him and he could concentrate on what was on the plate. A handful of peas, a dab of mashed potatoes, a tomato sliced into bleeding circles, a sprinkling of grated carrot, and no rice. White people are funny, he told himself. How can anyone fill himself with this? It doesn't form a lump like the food my mama makes. He washed it down with milk.

'Thank you, Annie,' he said as he pushed the glass aside. He sat fidgeting, impatient to be outside, away from the kitchen with its glossy, tiled floor and steel cupboards ducoed a clinical white to match the food-stacked refrigerator.

'I see you've finished.' The voice startled him. She held out an envelope containing the rand note — payment for his mother's weekly struggle over the wash tub. 'This is for you.' A five cent piece was dropped into his hand, a long fingernail raking his palm.

'Thank you, merrum.' His voice hardly audible.

'Tell your mother I'm going away on holiday for about a month and I'll let her know when I'm back.'

Then he was dismissed and her heels tapped out of the kitchen.

He nodded his head at the African maid who took an apple from a bowl bursting with fruit and handed it to him. He grinned his thanks and her responding smile bathed her face in light. He walked down the path finishing the apple with big bites.

The dog was after him before he reached the gate, its hot breath warming his heels. He turned and poked his toes into its face. It barked hoarsely in protest, a look of outrage on its face. He laughed delightedly at the expression which changed the dog's features into those of an old man.

'Let's see you do that again.' He waved his feet in

front of the pug's nose. The nose retreated and made an about-turn, waddling away with its dignity deflated by his affront.

As he walked, he mentally spent his five cents. I'll buy a penny drops, the sour ones that taste like limes, penny bull's eyes, a packet of sherbet with the licorice tube at the end of the packet, and a penny star toffees, red ones that turn your spit into blood.

His glands were titillated and his mouth filled with saliva. He stopped at the first shop and walked in.

Trays were filled with expensive chocolates and sweets of a type never seen in the jars on the shelves of the Indian shop on the corner where he stayed. He walked out without buying a thing.

His footsteps lagged as he reached the park. The nurse girls with their babies and prams were gone, their places occupied by old men who, with their hands holding up their stomachs, cast disapproving eyes over the confusion and clatter confronting them.

A ball was kicked perilously close to an old man, and the boy who ran after it stopped short as the old man raised his stick, daring him to come closer.

The rest of them called to the boy to get the ball. He edged closer and made a grab at it as the old man swung his cane. The cane missed the boy by more than a foot and he swaggered back, the ball held under his arm. Their game was resumed.

He watched them from the other side of the railings — the boys kicking the ball, the children cavorting on the grass, even the old men, senile on the seats; but most of all, he watched the children enjoying themselves with what was denied him, and his whole body yearned again to be part of them.

'Shit it!' He looked over his shoulder to see if anyone had heard him. 'Shit it!' he said louder. 'Shit it!

Shit it!'

His small hands impotently shook the tall railings towering above his head. It struck him that he would not be seeing the park for a whole month, that there would be no reason for him to pass it. Despair filled him. He had to do something to ease his anger. A bag filled with fruit peels was on top of the rubbish stacked in a waste basket fitted to a pole. He reached for it, threw it over the railings, and ran without waiting to see the result.

Out of breath three streets further, he slowed down, pain stabbing beneath his heart. The act had brought no relief, only intensified the longing. He was oblivious of the people passing, the hoots of the vehicles whose paths he crossed without thinking. And once, when he was roughly pushed aside, he did not even bother to look and see who had done it.

The familiar shrieks and smells told him that he was home. Even the Indian shop could not draw him out of his melancholy mood and he walked past it, his five cent piece unspent in his pocket.

A group of boys were playing with tyres on the pavement. They called to him but he ignored them and turned into a short side street. He mounted the flat stoep of a two-storey house with a facade that must once have been painted but had now turned a nondescript grey with the red brick underneath showing.

Beyond the threshold the room was dim. He walked past the scattered furniture with a familiarity that would have guided him blindfolded.

His mother was in the kitchen hovering over a pot perched on a pressure stove. He placed the envelope on the table. She put aside the spoon and stuck a finger under the flap of the envelope, tearing it in half. She placed the rand note in a spoutless teapot on the shelf.

'You hungry?'

He nodded his head. She poured him a cup of soup and added a thick slice of brown bread. Between bites of bread and sips of soup which scalded his throat, he told his mother that there would not be any washing coming during the week.

'Why? What the matter? What I do?'

'Nothing. Merrum say she go away for month. She let mama know she back.'

'What I do now?' Her voice took on a whine and her eyes strayed to the teapot containing the money. The whine hardened to reproach as she continued. 'Why don't she let me know she going away then I can look for another merrum?' She paused. 'I slave away and the pain never leave my back but it too much for her to let me know she go away. The money I get from her keep us nice and steady. How I go cover the hole?'

He wondered how the rand note he had brought helped to keep them nicely steady. There was no change in their meals. It was, as usual, not enough, and the only time they received new clothes was at Christmas.

'I must pay the burial, and I was going to tell Mr Lemonsky·to bring lino for the front room. I'm sick looking at the lino full of holes but I can forget now. With no money you got as much hope as getting wine on Sunday.'

He hurried his eating to get away from her words before they could soak into him, trapping him in the chair as the witness to his mother's miseries.

Outside, they were still playing with their tyres. He joined them half-heartedly. As he rolled the tyre his spirit was still in the park, on the swings. There was no barrier to his coming and he could do as he pleased. He was away from narrow streets and squawking children and speeding cars. He was in a place of green grass and red tubing and silver steel. The tyre rolled past him. He made no effort to grab it.

'Get the tyre!' 'You sleep?' 'Don't you want to play any more?'

He walked away ignoring their cries.

Rage boiled up inside him. Rage against the houses with streaked walls and smashed panes, filled by too many people; against the over-flowing garbage pails outside doors; the alleys and streets; and against a law he could not understand — a law that shut him out of the park.

He burst into tears. He swept his arms across his cheeks to check his weeping, then lowered his hands to peer at the boy confronting him.

'I think you cry!'

'Who say I cry? Something in my eye and I rub it.'

He pushed past and continued towards the shop. 'Cry baby!' the boy's taunt rang after him.

The shop's sole iron-barred window was crowded. Oranges were mixed with writing paper and dried figs were strewn on school slates. Clothing and crockery gathered dust. Across the window a cockroach made its leisurely way, antennae on the alert.

Inside, the shop was as crowded as the window. Bags covered the floor, leaving a narrow path to the till. The shopkeeper, an ancient Indian with a face tanned like cracked leather, leaned across the counter. 'Yes, boy?' He showed teeth scarlet with betel nut. 'Come'n, boy. What you want? No stand here all day.' His jaws worked at the nut held captive by his stained teeth.

He ordered penny portions of his selections, transferred the sweets to his pockets, threw the torn wrappings on the floor, and walked out. Behind him the Indian murmured grimly, jaws working faster.

One side of the street was in shadow. He sat with his back against the wall, savouring the last of the sun. Bull's-eye, peppermint, a piece of licorice — all lumped together in his cheek. For a moment the park was forgotten. He watched without interest the girl advancing.

'Mama say you must come'n eat.' She stared at his bulging cheek, one hand rubbing the side of her nose. 'Gimme.' He gave her a bull's eye which she dropped into her mouth between dabs at her nose.

'Wipe your snot!' he ordered her, showing his superiority. He walked past. She followed, sucking and sniffing. Their father was already seated at the table when they entered the kitchen.

'Must I always send somebody after you?' his mother asked.

He slipped into his seat and then hurriedly got up to wash his hands before his mother could find fault on another point. Supper was a silent affair except for the scraping of spoons across plates and an occasional sniff from his sister.

A thought came to his mind almost at the end of the meal. He sat, spoon poised in the air, shaken by its magnitude. Why not go to the park after dark? After it had closed its gates on the old men, the children, and the nurses with their prams! There would be no one to stop him.

He could think no further. He was light-headed with the thought of it. His mother's voice, as she related her day to his father, was not the steam that stung, but a soft breeze wafting past him, leaving him undisturbed. Then qualms troubled him. He had never been in that part of town at night. A band of fear tightened across his chest, contracting his insides, making it hard for him to swallow his food. He gripped his spoon tightly, stretching his skin across his knuckles.

I'll do it! I'll go to the park as soon as we're finished eating. He controlled himself with difficulty. He swallowed what was left on his plate and furtively watched to see how the others were faring. Hurry up! Hurry up!

He hastily cleared the table when his father pushed the last plate aside, and began washing up. Each piece of crockery was passed for drying to his sister whose sniffing kept pace with their combined operation.

The dishes done, he swept the kitchen and carried out the garbage bin.

'Can I go play, mama?'

'Don't let me have to send for you again.'

His father remained silent, buried behind the newspaper.

'Before you go,' — his mother stopped him — 'light the lamp and hang it in the passage.'

He filled the lamp with paraffin, turned up the wick and lit it. The light glimmered weakly through the streaked glass.

The moon, to him, was a fluorescent ball — light without warmth — and the stars were fragments chipped off it. Beneath street lights card games were in session. He sniffed the nostril-prickling smell of dagga as he walked past. Dim doorways could not conceal couples clutching at each other.

Once clear of the district, he broke into a trot. He did not slacken his pace as he passed through the downtown area with its wonderland shop windows.

His elation seeped out as he neared the park and his footsteps dragged.

In front of him was the park with its gate and iron railings. Behind the railings, impaled, was the notice board. He could see the swings beyond. The sight strengthened him. He walked over, his breath coming faster. There was no one in sight. A car turned a corner and came towards him, and he started at the sound of its engine. The car swept past, the tyres softly licking the asphalt.

The railings were icy-cold to his touch and the shock sent him into action. He extended his arms and with monkey-like movements pulled himself up to perch on top of the railings, then dropped on to the newly turned earth.

The grass was damp with dew and he swept his feet across it. Then he ran, the wet grass bowing beneath his bare feet. He ran towards the swings, the merry-go-round, the see-saw, the chute, his hands covering the metal.

Up the steps to the top of the chute. He stood outlined against the sky. He was a bird; an eagle. He flung himself down on his stomach, sliding swiftly. Wheeeeeee! He rolled over when he slammed onto the grass. He looked at the moon for an instant then propelled himself to his feet and ran for the steps of the chute to recapture that feeling of flight. Each time he swept down the chute, he wanted the trip never to end. He wanted to go on sliding, sliding, sliding.

He walked reluctantly past the see-saw, consoling himself with a push at one end to send it whacking down on the grass.

'Shit it!' he grunted as he strained to set the merry-go-round into action. Thigh tensed, leg stretched, he pushed. The merry-go-round moved. He increased his exertions and jumped on, one leg trailing at the ready to shove if it should slow down. The merry-go-round dipped and swayed. To keep it moving, he had to push more than he rode. Not wanting to spoil his pleasure, he jumped off and raced for the swings.

Feet astride, hands clutching silver chains, he jerked his body to gain momentum. He crouched like a runner then violently straightened. The swing widened its arc. It swept higher, higher, higher. It reached the sky. He could touch the moon. He plucked a star to pin to his breast. The earth was far below. No bird could fly as he. Upwards and onwards he went.

A light switched on in the hut at the far side of the park. It was a small patch of yellow on a dark square. The door opened and he saw a figure in the doorway. Then the door was shut and the figure strode towards him. He knew it was the attendant. A torch glinted brightly as it swung at his side.

He continued swinging.

The attendant came to a halt in front of him, out of reach of the swing's arc, and flashed his torch. The light caught him in mid-air.

'God dammit!' the attendant swore. 'I told you before you can't get on the swings.'

The rattle of the chains when the boy shifted his feet was the only answer he received.

'Why you come back?'

'The swings. I come back for the swings.'

The attendant catalogued the things denied them because of their colour. Even his job depended on their goodwill.

'Blerry whites! They get everything!'

All his feelings urged him to leave the boy alone, to let him continue to enjoy himself, but the fear that someone might see them hardened him.

'Get off! Go home!' he screamed, his voice harsh, his anger directed at the system that drove him against his own. 'If you don't get off, I go for the police. You know what they do to you.'

The swing raced back and forth.

The attendant turned and hurried towards the gate.

'Mama. Mama!' His lips trembled, wishing himself safe in his mother's kitchen, sitting next to the still-burning stove with a comic spread across his knees. 'Mama. Mama!' His voice mounted, wrenched from his throat, keeping pace with the soaring swing as it climbed the sky. Voice and swing. Swing and voice. Higher. Higher. Higher. Until they were one.

At the entrance of the park the notice board stood tall, its shadow elongated, pointing towards him.

11.41 to Simonstown

Near the station, propped up against a wall, was the man who had had both his legs amputated above the knees but whose impassive face showed that he had not lost his dignity as a man. He rested on the palms of his hands, in front of him a pile of newspapers. A brief flicker of his eyes was the only acknowledgement if more than the customary charge for a newspaper was dropped into his cap. The stairs at the top of the subway were guarded by a squad of ticket examiners clad in thick woollen uniforms.

Except for children, none of the passengers on the crowded platform showed any interest in the trains slithering to a halt at the opposite platform. The train pulled in — the 11.41 to Simonstown. 'Mowbray. Alle stasies Simonstad. Simonstown,' the ticket examiners bawled.

It was not a time for the niceties of behaviour. Elbow-gouging was the only way to get a seat. Otherwise it meant a long, unsettling stand with fingers curled around a shoulder strap. The carriage was packed and although all the windows were open, the built-in smell of third-class carriages was nostril-prickling. Only those new to third-class travel found the indefinable odours upsetting.

At each stop more passengers forced their way inside, turning the space between the two long benches running the length of the carriage into a market place of parcels, suitcases and squatting children. A puppy gave a yelp of pain as someone trod on its paw.

Conversation was loud and interspersed with belly-rumbling laughter. Bottles clinked merrily, signifying the start of the weekend. Those who could not wait until they reached home took out a spare bottle and drank deeply. Bottles were passed from hand to hand.

'Alle kaartjies! All tickets!' — the voice of authority. The signal for bottles to be hurriedly shoved into supermarket bags, only to be pulled out when the ticket examiner had made his exit. An inebriated fellow-traveller belched loudly each time the train jerked. Those seated on either side looked alarmed at each loud protestation. Others in the vicinity wondered how long it would take before an over-loaded stomach would weaken.

A series of hip-jolting jerks supplied the answer.

The result was not pleasing to the wearer of the off-white coat seated next to the very much sick-to-the-stomach traveller. The off-white coat was dyed by a torrent of greenish bile.

The wearer of the off-white coat raised a fist in retaliation but quickly withdrew as another torrent cascaded his way.

The 'What must be, must be' from a pipe-thin woman dangling from an overhead strap was not very consoling to the owner of the soiled garment, who glared ineffectively at her and the despoiler of his coat, dabbing at his mouth with a sheet of newspaper which he then spread on the floor to cover the remains of a liquid lunch.

'Wine is a mocker, and strong drink is raging. Whosoever is deceived thereby is not wise. That, my brothers and sisters, is found in the Book of Proverbs. And that is God's truth!' The words froze the drinkers and they sat with bottles poised in mid-air, eyes focused on the speaker. 'Yes, my friends. It is written in the bible that wine will make you as worthless as the swine driven into the sea. The drinkers of wine are like rotten fruit to be ploughed into the earth.'

The voice high-pitched as a boy soprano, the face smooth and unlined. Hair shaped into a widow's peak, two lines arrowing down his cheeks to flourish in a neatly-trimmed beard. His eyes sharp and piercing, stabbing at those he addressed, had the haughtiness of a camel. His tall, lean body moved with grace, lending an elegance to the drab olive raincoat he wore.

'Shit!' a drinker ejaculated.

'No, my friend. It is not shit,' the saviour of souls countered, waving his bible in front of the speaker, his eyes flashing a challenge to further disputants of the veracity of the word of the Lord.

'God so loved the world that He gave His only begotten son to save sinners. Is it too much to ask of you that you should give up wine?'

'But Jesus also made wine,' someone said defensively.

The plea was not worthy of a reply and the speaker was raked contemptuously by the piercing eyes of the preacher.

'It is said here in the bible, Matthew 6, verse 24: "No man can serve two masters; for either he will hate the one, and love the other." You cannot serve God and wine!'

In the short spell of silence that held sway the

adenoidal breathing of a youth with acne-scarred features scraped the air. His short-sleeved sweater proclaimed 'I Need Loving' in scarlet letters across his chest.

The preacher stepped back and turned his body aslant, coat twirling, chin raised imperiously and his eyes eloquent with the message delivered. His stance was that of an actor who has delivered a dramatic curtain speech. The histrionics of the occasion were not lost on him as he surveyed his not altogether captive audience, and if there had followed a burst of applause he would have accepted it as his due. A few loud amens showed that he had already won recruits to his cause.

The drinkers had not capitulated. Their dissension found voice in a short, fat man, the bags under his eyes testimony to his addiction to the vine.

'Who give you the right to preach?' he challenged. 'Is this your church?'

The preacher strode towards him, bible held aloft like a banner.

'As the Lord has sent his apostles to preach His word in the highways and the byways, so do I follow in the footsteps of the apostles. The church of God is wherever His word is spread.'

'That still don't give you the say-so to tell us what to do. We don't belong to your church.'

The preacher closed his eyes and bowed his head in prayer.

Another voice came to the defence of the drinkers. 'I know where he can shove up that crap he's giving us.'

The preacher twirled around fiercely to face this new attack.

'Mock not the word of God. For those who speak in blasphemous terms, their end will be bitter. Repent

before it is too late. Shed yourself of wine and drink
of the blood of the Lamb of God. Amen.'

His amen was fervently echoed by his followers.

Retreat Station: some of the adherents from both
camps departed. Buildings had thinned and fields
flanked the tracks, fields sprouting flowers and
vegetables. Nothing was needed to complete the
pastoral scene but cattle lowing, or a herd of horses
acanter with manes bannering the breeze. Then the
smell of ploughed earth changed to the smell of brine;
the fields of flowers were replaced by a pattern of
reeds, and boaters exploring the channels cutting
through the reeds.

The carriage was now divided into two camps. The
followers of the preacher were smaller in number but
their advocate was more eloquent in speech and
adroit in attack. The dissenters, though a large group,
erupted in solitary sorties that were all easily routed
by the preacher, who would then fire another broad-
side before the drinkers could marshal their reply.

Muizenberg pulled in more passengers. Fishermen
going through to Fish Hoek; domestic servants staying
at Noordhoek. As the train pulled out, one of the
girls spotted a companion of hers seated on a bench.

'Hey, Maria. You old jintoe!' she called. Maria, not
put out by the slur cast on her character, waved back
gaily and responded in a like manner; they laughed
friendly farewells.

A transistor radio entertained the new passengers.
A two-hundred-pound woman got up and went into a
shambling dance, flesh shifting in every direction. The
younger girls encouraged her with handclaps and
shrieks. 'Come'n,' she said, plucking at the sleeves of
two fishermen. Unable to keep up with her gyrating
they retired to their seats to replenish themselves

with wine.

She hoisted her dress to her thighs, revealing knee-caps the size of chamber pots, and climaxed her dance by grasping the slender pole shooting from floor to ceiling and swinging around it like a grotesque queen of the maypole. The fishermen complimented her with ribaldry.

The preacher's eagerness to engage this new group of desecraters of the law of God was emphasised by his words.

'Drunkenness, revellings and such like, of which I forewarn you, that they who practise such things shall not inherit the Kingdom of God.' He flipped open the pages of the bible to show further proof of the error of their ways. 'There are only two roads in life. The broad and the narrow. The broad road is filled with those partaking of the pleasure of the flesh and the world. The narrow road has but few travellers. For that is the road to eternal happiness.'

A young man, broad of shoulder, moved towards the preacher. Around his neck was draped a silken, tasselled scarf. A copper band glittered at an ear. He planted himself opposite the preacher's band.

'You, preacher. You listen to me,' he said arrogantly. 'I know all the roads. I travel all of them, and all roads the same. They all lead to one place. And that's hell! All of us, we end up there. You too, you and your hymn-singing lot!'

The drinkers were jubilant. 'That's right. Tell him!' they prompted their champion. 'He don't pay for what we drink. It's our own sweat.'

The preacher's followers looked expectantly at the preacher for the words that would vanquish his adversary.

The preacher looked at his attacker, measuring his

worth as an opponent.

'You are wrong, my brother.'

'I'm not your brother. My mother didn't lay with every man.'

The preacher shook his head in silent reprimand at the interruption.

'No, my brother. You are wrong. Man has an immortal soul, and by following in the footsteps of the Lord, he shall find his way to heaven on the day of judgement after we have been judged. It is not too late, my brother. Kneel here in prayer with me and your soul will yet find redemption, because the Lord is merciful to the lambs that have strayed from His flock.'

The offer of salvation was spurned.

The preacher ordered his congregation to pray for a lost soul. The congregation dutifully bowed their heads. The commencement of their prayer tapped a flow of vituperation.

The preacher's face reflected his serenity. He had found his Calvary. Each curse was a nail impaling him on his cross. He clasped his hands over his bible and held it to his breast.

The ticket examiner disturbed the tableau as he approached the preacher's castigator. 'You're going to have trouble with me if you don't stop your swearing.'

The preacher's coterie smiled their approval.

The examiner's reprimand had wilted the spirit of the boozers' brigade. Their champion was not cowed however, and after the examiner's exit he resumed battle.

'I know all your tricks. So don't come up all holy-holy for me. You no better than any of us. You sweet-Jesus us with your mouth and your eyes lead our women to your bed.'

He raised a gasp of outrage from the preacher's followers, which the preacher stilled with a flutter of hands. A middle-aged woman with ample bosom, heading three others cast in similar mould, and in whose midst sheltered a tiny old man, expostulated in shocked tones: 'Have you no shame? You talking to a man of God!'

'Ask him if he know what it is to be converted, a child of God,' said another of the bosomy ladies, nudging the old man whose wrinkled, skinny neck swivelled from side to side in his wide collar.

The old man, beady eyes flickering at the young man on the opposite seat, drew in his neck like a tortoise, his bobbing adam's apple evidence of his agitation. The ferocity displayed by the young man deterred him.

Then the presence of the preacher lent strength to the old man and his reedy voice rasped: 'If you had walked the ways of those converted, your tongue would not play you false like a serpent.'

The woman's section of those assured of the salvation of their souls looked with approval on the old man, who was safeguarded by their bulk.

The old man's admonition was too much. The young man responded with another explosion of expletives. The carriage was hushed, all eyes on the examiner who, at the first curse, had stopped in his task of collecting tickets. Body stiff with fury, he stalked towards the offender.

'I told you I didn't want to hear any more filth from you,' he said as he grabbed hold of the offender's scarf and pulled him to his feet.

The drinkers sat crestfallen as they watched their champion marched to the guard's van.

The preacher spoke quietly, like soft rain, then the

words came hard and fast as hail hammering the
stubborn earth. 'It is said in Proverbs 23, verse 30 to
32: "They that tarry long at the vine, they that go to
seek mixed wine. Look not upon the wine when it is
red, when it giveth its colour in the cup, when it goes
down smoothly, at the last it biteth like a serpent,
and stingeth like an adder." Brothers and sisters, the
word of God is Law.'

Hallelujahs showered like offerings dropped on an
altar.

'Wonderful the ways of the Lord,' one of the
women exclaimed. 'He think he can mock the word
of God, and see what happens to him!'

The bosomy quartet started singing and the hymn
was taken up by the others. The old man's voice was
a trembly quaver. Their singing was punctuated by an
occasional grumble. The drinker who had first challenged the preacher's prerogative to sound a sermon
sat hunched up, cradling a bottle from which he took
sips in between venom-tipped glances at the preacher
who stood unperturbed and triumphant.

The rails were laid flat on the sand; the sea almost
within touching distance. Simonstown, with naval
ships riding at anchor. A white gull traced its route
against the blue of the sky. The preacher and his congregation departed, singing a paean of praise to their
Maker, and a condemnation on those who sought to
thwart His work. He led his willing flock across the
sand to wash away all signs of visible sin in the waters
of the sea of Galilee.

A Clash of Colour

Aware of their scrutiny, he shifted his buttocks un-
easily on the bench, raised his head, and looked
towards the counter. Their eyes pinned him and he
hurriedly lowered his gaze, swallowed deeply and
wiped his perspiring palms on his thighs. Thabu, next
to him, was not affected by the intimidation that had
cowed him.

He was still bewildered by his presence in the
charge office. Their two companions were on the
other side of the partition.

They were walking towards the station when the
police van drew up next to them.

'Where are you going?'

No one answered the policeman seated at the window on their side. The question was repeated and
he saw that it was directed at the two companions he
had met at the party during the course of the night.

'We're going to the station,' Reuben answered.

'Where do you come from?'

'Why?'

He turned startled to Thabu, who had spoken.

The policeman looked at Thabu and a ridge of
muscle formed on his jawbone.

'We come from a party,' Ian interjected.

'Party?' The policeman looked at them in turn — a coloured, an African, and two whites. 'You come from a party?' He expressed his incredulity and the spacing of the words gave him time to rationalise four men of different racial groups attending the same party.

'Is going to a party against the law?' Thabu asked, voice tinged with sarcasm.

The policeman jerked open the van door as if it was hot metal, and stepped in front of Thabu.

'What did you say?'

'Have they passed a law that parties are illegal, or does it only apply to Sundays?'

The mockery in Thabu's words was reflected upon his face.

The policeman raised his hand as if to lash out at Thabu then glanced at Reuben and Ian, ignoring him.

'Where's your pass?'

'At home.'

The policeman's hands flitted to Thabu's pockets like hawks plummeting upon doves. Thabu made no resistance as his pockets were turned inside out, the contents dropping to the ground.

A pamphlet was withdrawn from an inside pocket. A black clenched fist took up the top portion of the pamphlet. Underneath it black letters stated, 'ACG Newsletter'.

The policeman flipped open the pamphlet and scrutinised its contents, his eyes widening as he read.

'Kyk hier!' he said, thrusting the pamphlet through the window to the policeman behind the wheel. 'Look what this kaffir's got on him.'

The policeman turned and jerked Thabu by the sleeve towards the back of the van. Thabu pulled free and picked up the contents of his pockets strewn on the ground. The policeman made another threatening gesture.

Thabu smiled at him before being thrust into the back of the van.

'See that you get to the station,' was the policeman's parting command as the van pulled away.

'What was that pamphlet all about?' Reuben asked him.

'It's an ACG newsletter.'

Reuben and Ian showed their puzzlement in the questioning stare they accorded him.

'What does ACG stand for?'

'Azanian Cultural Group.'

'Is it banned?' Ian asked hesitantly.

He shook his head. 'It's not banned, but a number of its members have been picked up by the Special Branch.'

'Are you a member?'

He looked at Reuben, then said almost inaudibly: 'No. I don't belong to any such groups.'

'And Thabu?'

'I don't know. We work together and he's often given me ACG literature, but has never said that he was a member.'

'What are you going to do about it?' Ian asked, shifting responsibility for Thabu's welfare on to him.

'What can I do about it?' he replied plaintively.'

'Do you know anyone else who belongs to ACG?' Reuben asked.

He shook his head.

'There must be someone who would be able to help,' Reuben continued. 'We just can't leave it like this.'

'I'll phone my boss.'

'Do you think he'll be able to help Thabu?'

'He'll know what to do. Twice, when Thabu was in trouble with his pass, the boss cleared it up for him,' he said, feeling better, as if the responsibility of aiding Thabu had been removed from him. 'Let's go back. I can use the phone.'

He looked at their faces as they retraced their footsteps. He had met them for the first time the previous evening. He had been surprised when Thabu had suggested that he accompany him to the party. Normally their relationship was confined to office hours. They would walk together towards the station at the end of the day's work, where they boarded different trains. He knew very little of Thabu's life outside the office. It was the first time that he had gone to a party where the guests were a racial mixture. His approach was diffident, content to let Thabu do the talking, and amazed at how he could dominate a conversation: a side of his friend that was new to him. Thabu had treated Reuben and Ian, and the other whites present, with a casual ease that he envied. They walked into the same police van as they turned a corner. The van glided to a halt in front of them.

'So, you're going to the station,' the policeman said, opening the cab door and advancing towards them. 'I think you better join your kaffir friend.'

'Are we under arrest?' Reuben asked.

The policeman did not bother to reply, moving them to the back of the van and slamming the door upon them.

The ride to the police station was a short one and he was still trying to sort out his confused thoughts when they were deposited in the charge office. Reuben and Ian were moved to the other side of the partition that divided the charge office into two sections. Thabu sat sprawled on a bench stretching from the counter to the door. The policeman indicated that he should join him.

The pamphlet was circulating among the policemen and their eyes charged aggressively from the pamphlet to Thabu and himself.

A finger beckoned and he rose and stood in front of the counter.

'Name?'

He looked at the three stripes on the arm resting in front of him.

'Frank Williams,' he said diffidently.

'Address?'

He responded to the rest of the questions in the same diffident manner. His interrogator looked up and appraised him when he answered that he was a department head in the spares division.

'What's your salary?'

'R520.'

He received another searching look. There was a change of tone in the rest of the questions, as if the revelation of his salary and job position had raised him in their esteem.

'Can I phone my boss?'

'I'll ask the commandant when he comes,' the sergeant said in not unkindly tones.

He observed the sergeant talking to the other policeman behind the counter and pointing at him as he resumed his seat. They looked at him with renewed interest.

'What's going to happen?' he asked Thabu fearfully.

'Don't you worry,' Thabu assured him.

A rapping was heard above their heads. They looked upwards to see Reuben's head hovering.

'Could I have your pipe?' Reuben asked.

'Sure,' Thabu replied, reaching into his pocket and

passing the pipe to Reuben.

'What about matches?'

Reuben lit up, sending smoke signals ceilingwards.

'Ta,' he said, dropping the matches into Thabu's lap.

'Sies! Did you see that? Smoking a kaffir's pipe!'

'What sort of a white man is he?'

'Kaffir boetie!'

Thabu nudged him in the ribs, an amused smile on his face.

A woman with two small girls dragging at her skirt entered the charge office. She halted in front of the counter, looking enquiringly at the seated policemen. No one took any notice of her questioning stare and their silence intimidated her. The girls eyed their surroundings curiously, their gaze settling on the two men seated on the bench, then moving on.

The woman stood waiting patiently to draw the attention of the policemen whose eyes flickered past her as if she did not exist. The girls sank down on their haunches and whispered their observations conspiratorially. Their voices grew louder and their mother bent over to hush them.

'Ja, what are you here for?'

The woman's head jerked up in alarm.

'My man put us out,' she stammered at the policeman leaning across the counter. 'Me and the children.'

'Is he drunk?'

She nodded.

'So, now we've got to put up with your man's drinking!'

She hung her head as if found guilty of her husband's intoxication.

'Go home and tell him the baas at the police station says he'll find himself in trouble if he doesn't let you in.'

The woman gratefully mumbled her thanks as she hurried from the charge office, her children trotting at her side.

'The law's will be done,' Thabu said drily.

An elderly white man, skin pink and polished, wearing an open-necked shirt, black blazer and white trousers, entered the charge office. The policemen behind the counter rose as if a judge had entered a court room.

'Môre, Kommandant.'

The station commander waved paternally at them before disappearing down a passage.

The sergeant who had questioned him rose, carrying a sheaf of questionnaires, and followed his superior. When he returned, he told him that he could make one telephone call.

He stood fidgeting as he dialled. His employer's voice grated in his ear. 'Morning, Mr Wilson,' he said servilely. 'I'm phoning from Wynberg police station. We've been picked up, Thabu and me. I don't know what the charge is.' He looked at Thabu. 'They found a pamphlet in Thabu's pocket.' His employer swore at the other end. 'Sergeant, my boss wants to speak to you.'

He passed the telephone to the sergeant who had stood listening to the conversation.

'I'm afraid I can't tell you,' the sergeant said. 'A political pamphlet was found on the kaf . . . er, bantu,' the sergeant corrected himself, 'and they were together . . . . It looks like a case for the Special Branch. . . . . Certainly.'

The telephone was passed back to him.

'Mr Wilson? . . . No, I don't know anything about it . . . . I'll tell him . . . . Sir, please, sir. Get me out of this.'

He reluctantly replaced the receiver, murmured his thanks to the sergeant, and joined Thabu.

Thabu looked at him quizzically.

'The boss says he'll try to get a lawyer.' He added hesitantly, 'Thabu, that pamphlet, is it banned?'

'No, it's not.'

'Then why are they keeping . . . us?'

He had almost said 'me'.

'I told you not to worry. Everything will work out fine. They going to ask a lot of stupid questions then they let us go.'

He could not altogether accommodate the confidence displayed in Thabu's words. From within the passage a door slammed and he shivered uncontrollably.

'Catch,' Reuben called and the pipe fell between them. Thabu picked it up, held it aloft then filled it with tobacco. He puffed unconcernedly as disgust registered on the faces of the policemen.

The commandant emerged from his office. 'Tell Sergeant van Tonder I'm in my office when he comes. I hope he's not going to keep me waiting. There's a bowls competition I'm taking part in this afternoon.' He gave a cursory glance at the two men on the bench.

His breath quickened. He had heard of Sergeant van Tonder, or rather, he had seen the name often in reports of blacks detained by the Special Branch. He had read that people were detained for an undisclosed number of days without being brought to court or having access to a lawyer to represent them. His dread increased.

Jesus, why did I go to the party with Thabu? Normally, he would have taken his girl-friend to a cinema, but Thabu's talk of whites being present at the party had intrigued him. He had visualised white girls being present and had pictured himself on intimate terms with them: a thought that was often in his mind when he looked at the white female staff at the office. Lord, don't let them hold me. He dared not think further of the consequences of his detention.

'Thabu, have you been in jail before?'

Then he remembered Thabu's pass offences.

'Every African has been in jail at least once,' Thabu said matter-of-factly. 'It's part of growing up.'

His fears prodded further questioning.

'What's it like?'

'Hell!' Thabu said quietly. 'In jail they add the finishing touches to the process that makes you a no-man. They take away your identity. Your name is replaced by a swear word and blows used as speech. But it's not only they who turn you into a beast. It's also our own kind. I've seen men old as my father turn into whimpering children under the blows of the dogs who do their masters' work. And in the darkness of the cell, the weeping of men who have been turned into women.'

Thabu's words evoked a scene that was frightening.

A man strode into the charge office. 'Môre, Sergeant van Tonder. The commandant is in his office.'

He looked up into a pair of cold, grey eyes that did not reflect emotion and his apprehension chilled him.

The commandant and Sergeant van Tonder re-appeared a few minutes later, the latter with the sheaves of questionnaires in his possession.

'Reg dan, van Tonder. I'm going home for lunch.' The commandant patted his old man's paunch. 'I must build up strength for the tournament this afternoon.'

Sergeant van Tonder walked the commandant to the door, stood watching as he got into his car, then turned towards the counter.

'Who brought them in?'

'Me, sergeant.'

'Is this the only thing?' Sergeant van Tonder fluttered the pamphlet.

'I think so, sergeant.'

'Didn't you search them, man?'

The policeman blushed, and in his haste to make amends clambered across the counter and lumbered in their direction.

The policeman's hands went through his pockets before he could protest and his possessions were piled into a heap on the bench.

'That one, as well,' Sergeant van Tonder indicated Thabu.

'But I've searched him already, sergeant.'

'Man, search him again,' Sergeant van Tonder said patiently.

The woman who had been in previously to complain about her husband made her appearance and stood nervously aside as the policeman pulled Thabu to his feet. The two girls accompanying her scuttled to her side and peeked fearfully at the scene confronting them.

'His belt, man!' Sergeant van Tonder admonished the policeman. 'Must I still teach you your job?'

'Bloody kaffir!' the policeman muttered angrily.

The belt slipped from the loops and ripped open the fly causing Thabu's trousers to concentrate around his ankles.

He looked at the woman, who averted her eyes, at the children stifling their giggles in their mother's skirt.

The items from their pockets were placed into separate envelopes. Sergeant van Tonder added the information to the questionnaires and re-entered the commandant's office.

He looked at his friend's impassive face, his eyes slithering away in confusion as Thabu returned his gaze.

'Thabu,' he whispered brokenly, 'what can I say?' The expression on Thabu's face excluded further communication. He shrugged his shoulders helplessly, his outstretched hand falling limply to his side.

Then Thabu gripped his shoulder and he turned to find that the bleak expression that had guarded those features had relaxed. Now he saw a lop-sided grin and understanding eyes.

He tried to draw comfort from the strength Thabu emitted.

The policeman stood in front of them. 'Kom, kaffir,' he said, pulling at Thabu's shoulder.

He watched, feeling sick, as Thabu and the policeman walked in the direction of the commandant's office.

He sweated through the time of Thabu's absence, trying to visualise what would be happening in the commandant's office. He knew that he did not have Thabu's strength to stand up to whatever form Sergeant van Tonder's questioning would take. His fear isolated him and he had the feeling that he was in a wasteland with an unknown force waiting to swoop upon him and bear him to destruction. A moan escaped his lips and he raised his hand to his mouth.

'Come'n.' The policeman stood in front of him.

He rose unsteadily, not daring to ask what had happened to Thabu.

The policeman knocked at the commandant's

door, opened it, and nudged him forward.

The cold eyes of Sergeant van Tonder engulfed him and he advanced on trembling limbs.

Jesus Christ, help me!